# IMMINENT SHIFT

# IMMINENT SHIFT

## *in human consciousness and awakening to the ET Phenomenon*

Harrison Viers Newberry

ISBN: 9798218521677

# CONTENTS

# FOREWORD

*Imminent Shift* was an inspiring page-turner!

When I was asked by the author to write a foreword, I was honored and excited. I have known Harrison and his wife for thirty years. We have traveled many journeys together. So I thought I knew what to expect before reading his manuscript. But it contained so much more than I could have ever imagined.

My father was a Baptist deacon, so I had a strict Christian upbringing. Over the years I remained true to the interpretations of the Bible. I admit that I always had questions on several areas of the New Testament but was afraid to approach. I hesitated to waver from the teachings I had grown up with since childhood.

Harrison tied it all together in a way that gave me permission to want to explore. In fact, I am anxious to seek out much of the research he mentioned in his book and look for more information. I also realized I need to look within myself and try to awaken my own spirit more.

In the infinite universe, how could we possibly think this is the only planet with intelligent life? I do not know how anyone could question the presence of alien life after reading the long list of facts presented in these pages. In the past, I never allowed myself to contemplate this. When I read of the many government documents and the countless eyewitness accounts, I was compelled to accept it as reality.

I, too, have heard from several sources of the coming shift. I am sure I am not alone in admitting this has made me uneasy. The shift of the earth—and the how and why it is happening—has been verified by many brilliant scientists. Just as Harrison describes here, I am convinced it is happening now. His focus on the evolution of our consciousness does appear to be the answer. We must awaken now.

I have determined the shift will bring into existence a new and glorious reality that I imagine as magnificent. I am convinced this will not only occur but also very soon.

I am enjoying my exploration into my unknown.
*Great job, Harrison!*

—Donna Britt

# PROLOGUE

The greatest story in human history is happening now. Sadly, there are so many people worldwide who are almost completely unaware of it. The earth itself is shifting. Our consciousness is evolving, and disclosure on the alien UAP phenomenon is imminent. We are on the cusp of a new reality. There have been countless books written on spirituality and human consciousness. In addition, there is a like number of books on the UFO/UAP story. This book is being written to connect the two stories together. I am convinced that when we have open contact with our alien visitors, the answers we have been seeking will be much more spiritual than about the nuts and bolts of technology. In truth, these two stories are not only connected but also the same.

After conducting thousands of hours of research and investigation, I have concluded that there are two separate realities being lived by humans on this planet. One is what I call the "normal reality," which we all know. However, there is a separate reality being lived in secrecy worldwide. This is the deep, dark, and covert world of the secret space force. It consists of covert military and intelligence agencies, and the military industrial complex. Many refer to those in control as the Cabal. They are traveling off planet, have trade agreements with extraterrestrials, and are making trillions of dollars every year. This has been taking place for several decades now.

My intent in writing this book is threefold. One is to help you to become aware of this because a disclosure event is coming soon. They are painfully aware this cannot be kept secret much longer. They know these two realities must come together. The experts say this is imminent. My second intention is to make you aware that the earth is now going through a "Shift," due to the poles moving at the earth's core and increased solar activity. This could be catastrophic. It has happened several times in the history of the planet, and experts say it is that time again. The third intent is to help humanity to awaken and ascend. Our solar system is now moving in alignment with the center of the galaxy. This means we are receiving a much higher frequency of energy. This will raise our vibration, hopefully into the fourth harmonic density. We are evolving from a 3D reality into the 4D, and then the 5D. Ultimately, what this means is that we are evolving into a more spiritual reality, a love-based frequency, and away from a fear based one.

Most everyone knows that humanity cannot continue the path we have been traveling. Every day we see the chaos, wars, crime, and violence. The world is full of fear, anger, depression, drug addiction, and suicide. We must awaken. We must evolve in consciousness. I know many say, "But what can we do about it, insofar as this shift?" We can make a huge difference if we do it collectively. We must get enough people to awaken, to form a critical mass, and together, we can make this shift a happy one. There are many in the know who have a very positive outlook. If enough of us awaken, we will move into a new reality on earth that most of us can barely imagine. A world without chaos, without hatred, and into a world of love.

This is the truth and where we are today. If we fail to awaken, I shudder to think what will occur. I wish I had a date, but no one knows. The best minds, quantum physicists, and many brilliant people agree on one thing; it is imminent. We all have free will. I cannot tell anyone what to believe or to do. We are focused on our own little realities. As one government insider said, "This is all coming, and when it happens, there are going to be many of you that wish you had paid attention." Otherwise, you will be confronted with a new reality with no understanding of how to navigate and care for your families. None of us can escape what is coming and very soon.

This book is written in two parts, A and B. Part A is about awakening from within ourselves, becoming aware of who we truly are. Ultimately, it is about human evolution of consciousness. Part B is about awakening to the universe we live in. Perhaps most important, it is about understanding how all of humanity has been lied to for over seven decades. Not only are we not alone in the cosmos, but we also have never been.

I am aware that this book will draw some controversy and ridicule. However, all my family and friends know I am a very honest and spiritual man. I am seventy-four years of age, way past trying to fool anyone. I ask that before you reject what I have written here, you do your own research. It is all available to you. Not one of us can hide from truth. This book is intended as my legacy to my family, friends, and humanity. In time, I know that everything contained here will be vindicated. I beg of you to hear, to awaken, and above all, to keep an open mind.

# PART A

# 1

## INTRODUCTION

My wife Maggie and I have awakened many mornings with a feeling of impending doom. Although it is difficult to describe, it seems to be more of a sense that something bad is going to happen. I then began interviewing countless numbers of people: friends, family, business associates, etcetera. It was not long before I realized that we were not alone in this feeling. The world we live in is filled with so much fear, manifesting as anger, greed, and negativity. I know there is a better way to live. Everyone knows the symptoms and that things are getting worse. We all feel powerless to change any of this. When I asked all those individuals what they believed the solution to be, I was happy to hear the same answer, again and again. They all said we must return to God. I was not surprised at this answer from most people. However, I was shocked when I heard it from some who had never been believers in anything spiritual. I certainly agreed with this, but I have learned the true answer goes much deeper. We must awaken, evolve in consciousness, and discover our true selves. Most every theologian, spiritual guru, and quantum physicist are fully aware of this. There are discussions taking place daily, worldwide, on this topic. If you listen closely to our media, you will hear the word *consciousness* being used constantly. This makes me grateful, but the flip side of it is that there are so many who do not understand the true meaning of the word. One does not need to be a spiritual guru, nor a scientist, to know that humanity cannot continue the path we have been on. I never thought I would live to see the day when science and religion would again be rejoined. That day has arrived. Millions of people all over the world are now awakening. This is the most important thing you can ever do, and it is critical that we do so. When we do evolve into the fourth harmonic and arrive in a new reality, the beauty will be beyond our wildest dreams. Can you imagine a world free of war, violence, poverty, etcetera, and full of love, happiness, and joy? If you are waiting on the government and the politicians to fix things, it will never happen. They are a huge part of the problem, not the solution. We, humans, must accept responsibility for our own destiny and cease giving our free will to the elite. Once we do, the symptoms will automatically resolve themselves. This gave me hope, but knowing people, I thought there is no way that some people will awaken. Then, I learned it is not necessary that every person awaken. We just must reach a critical mass. I just do not know what percentage of the population constitutes a critical mass. The good news is that millions of us have already awakened, and millions more soon will be. Franky, I cannot wait. I see a new reality without hate. A reality where already existing technologies will change everything; overunity energy devices, medical technology that will at least double the average human lifespan, antigravity cars, a clean atmosphere, and clean oceans, and the list is endless. I know some of you will think this is impossible, that it cannot happen. I am here to tell you that not only can it happen but it also will. We are not that far away, if everyone will just awaken and start pressing our politicians to disclose the truth, that we are not alone in the cosmos. These technologies already exist to bring about every change I just mentioned. They are held in secret, available only to the elite.

The earth has gone through many cycles, many resets. Among all the experts, we are at the end of a cycle now. We are at the end of an era, and a word I ask you to pay close attention to is *shift*. The earth is going through a shift. The poles are shifting, which could wipe out all life. This is not some scare tactic. It has happened before. Everyone on earth knows about the great flood. Christians know of the Noah's ark story, but similar stories exist in every culture and religion on earth. This happened somewhere around twelve thousand years ago, during the "Younger Dryas" period, the last ice age. Many experts say it is not a matter of if, but when, it will happen again. Nothing in our future is certain. There are only probabilities. The planet Earth is traveling through space at one hundred thousand miles per hour. The universe is expanding. Our Milky Way Galaxy is shifting. Our solar system is now moving to an alignment with the equator of our galaxy. We are receiving high frequency energy that is now shifting our consciousness. We humans are going through a "shift" as I am writing this story. This is why so many of us are awakening. As time speeds up, this awakening of human consciousness will continue to increase.

I have discovered that most of us, myself included, are so self-absorbed with just trying to feed our families and keep roofs over our heads, we have fallen asleep. We have failed to pay attention to the bigger picture. It is easier to just follow the crowd and believe what we have been told. This does not make us bad people. I know my mom and dad would have never have knowingly told me anything that was not true. I also do not believe my teachers would have ever intentionally misinformed me. In addition, I certainly do not claim any superior intellect. I simply was placed on a spiritual path several decades ago. It took years of tiny little steps for me to begin to awaken to the truth. I am nothing special, but through a series of tragedies in my early life, it became critical for me to awaken, or else. When I stepped back to view the bigger picture, I began to realize my parents, teachers, and mentors had taught me what they had been taught. I began to realize that we had all missed something of great importance. That was the fact that we are not what we thought we were, that we are so much more. There is no arrogance in that comment. Every single one of us is far more than we have been told and believed ourselves to be. In retrospect, I have wasted so much of my life living an illusion. I rigorously followed a spiritual path, including the teachings of Jusus Christ. I experienced moments of great inner peace and love. Yet I would always revert to my old patterns of living. I knew I had to be missing something but had no idea what that was. I kept digging deeper, reading everything I could get my hands on. I received a lot of training in various disciplines, from mind control to shamanism. I wrote about much of this in detail in my book *Shining Bear*. I have done thousands of hours in research and spoken to thousands of people. I finally arrived at a conclusion, which is the only thing I am sure of is that I am not sure of anything. Knowledge is both good and important, but nothing can replace direct experience. My Christian practices have all been based on belief, in faith, but I asked myself this question: "Could it be possible to experience the divine personally?" I began to do some research into the origins of various religions. What soon became evident is that at the core of most all the world's main religions, I found the same basic truths. In the beginning, hundreds, even thousands, of years ago, they were teaching methods for people to directly confront the divine. I was both stunned and amazed. I then asked, What happened to change this? The common thread is that churches were built. The church became the go-between from us to God. Man became involved, and so did the pursuit of power and money. As I became aware of this, it certainly got my attention. I wanted to directly experience God. This is where I went down the rabbit hole. I had to realize that I needed to unlearn some things. Next, I had to understand the true meaning of "Know thyself." I intend to delve into each of these topics, the question of whether we are alone in the universe, and more, in the following chapters.

Before I started writing this book, I shared with my wife, and some very close friends, what the subject matter would consist of. Every one of them cautioned me, pointing out these topics will be considered controversial to several people. Of course I understood this. I want every reader to know that I am not telling anyone what to believe. God gave all free will. I only ask you to keep an open mind. There are several topics included here that initially shocked me. I rejected them outright in the beginning. This is why I understand how this will hit some people hard. I have always believed the truth has a ring to it. I simply followed the ringing and began investigating. Every detail I write here is backed up by countless numbers of scientists, researchers, and witnesses. I quickly discovered one cannot simply read a pamphlet, or an article, or watch a single interview, to discover the truth. I have read mountains of books, listened to thousands of hours of interviews, and had years of personal direct experience to arrive at the conclusions you will read about here. My prayer is that this book will assist every reader in personal growth. I certainly do not claim to have all the answers to the topics herein. What I do know is that our world and our reality are shifting. This is happening right now, and no human on earth can escape this truth. I beg of you to wake up and start paying close attention. If we should fail, the best thing that could happen is that we will be taken back into the bronze age, or even worse.

# 2

---

## END-TIMES

---

In my first draft of this book, I was going to save this chapter for last. I then realized I wanted to place it up front. We all need to understand there is a sense of urgency, that the clock is running out on us. I have listened to many experts say we have been controlled for centuries. We have been almost entirely focused on the physical world around us, just survival. Many of us are suffering and living in some form of fear. Some experts say this control is a result of an extraterrestrial race known as the Draco Reptilian or the Arkon. Others say it is the small group of humans, the Cabal, with most of the wealth and power. Others say it is both, which I tend to agree with.

All over the world, religious leaders are saying we are now living in the "end-times." If you read the book of Revelation in the Bible, virtually all the signs and symptoms are there. These prophecies are from over two thousand years ago. Whether you believe in the Bible or not, you cannot deny that every prophecy has come true. Although I had studied other religions over the years, I only recently discovered that they all have end-time prophecies. Not only do the major religions have these beliefs and teachings, but they are also present in the spiritual teachings of the Indigenous peoples of the world. Every one of them speak of a "return" of a Jesus type of figure. This was, and is true, with the Mayans, Hopi, the Inca, and other Indigenous people in Africa and Australia. In my book *Shining Bear*, I shared the stories of my journeys into the mountains and jungles of Peru. I had learned of a small group of shamans, the spiritual leaders of the Inca. They were known as the Quero. In 1532, the Spanish conquistadores invaded the Inca empire. The Quero had seen them in visions of the approaching event. They knew they were coming and that there was nothing they could do to stop it. So they escaped and went up into one of their holy mountains, at altitudes of sixteen thousand feet and above. They lived there for over five hundred years. No one knew they were there. In fact, it was a myth even among the Quechua people, which we call the Inca. However, it was prophesied that they would return when the time approached for a new era to begin. They came off the mountain in 1994. A friend and mentor of mine, Dr. Alberto Villoldo, was present, and I have a video of the event. Later, I met with these incredible souls. Imagine meeting people who had never seen a car, a telephone, much less a cell phone, nor even a globe of the world. Yes, we could call them ancient, but when I looked into their eyes, it was what I could imagine it would be like to look into the eyes of Jesus Christ. I saw nothing but pure love and total peace. While they did not possess any of what we would call formal education, they were the wisest people I have ever met, from a spiritual perspective. I was blessed to have set in several ceremonies with them. They spoke of the coming shift, of the earth and of humanity. They returned to help us prepare and to evolve spiritually.

In early 2012, there were thousands of people who believed the world would end on December 21, 2012. This was the end of the Mayan calendar. I remember stories in the media of people preparing for the end of the world. We all know that time passed, and we are still here. I had forgotten about this until a few months ago. I was watching an interview of David Adair on Gaia TV. David may be the most brilliant man I have ever listened to. By the time he was six years old, he had read over six hundred books in the public library. I am talking about books on advanced topics like math, physics, quantum physics, and everything in science one can imagine. By age sixteen, he had read, and absorbed, thousands of books and had begun developing his own theories in theoretical physics. He was discovered by General Curtis LeMay and began working on projects for the military. In this interview, he shared the most remarkable story most of us have never heard of. He said that on July 23, 2012, there were three corona mass ejections, commonly known as CMEs, heading directly for Earth. These are huge balls of hot plasma, each the size of Mount Everest, as he described. Had they hit us, scientists said that within six months, every human on earth would have been dead. Ironically, this would have corresponded perfectly with the end of the Mayan calendar, December 21, 2012. So it would appear the Mayans were right. So why were we never told? Our government knew, as did many other governments around the world. NASA knew, and so did NOAH. In fact, our fearless leaders were holding an "open house" that day at Mount Weatherby in Virginia. This is a huge underground facility large enough to hold everyone who attends the State of the Union address and their combined families. David is a hoot, laughing about our fearless leaders running for cover and leaving the rest of us out to burn. These CMEs, three in a row, balls of hot plasma at thousands of degrees, were on a trajectory to hit Earth dead center. We all know this did not occur, so what happened? Well, at the last minute, something bumped them, shifting their trajectory just enough to miss us. They had traveled ninety-three million miles in about eighteen hours, just below the speed of light. They went between us and the moon, about 110,000 miles out, which is nothing compared to the distance they had traveled. We certainly did not have the technology to do this. David referred to an interview of a deep, covert military man, by journalist Linda Moulton Howell. This man said there was a huge spaceship parked just outside our atmosphere that saved us. Whether you or I believe this, the fact remains that something bumped them. We have no idea who it was. David said he would love to know so we could at least send them flowers. I agree; someone intervened that day and saved us. After learning of this, I immediately went online and looked it up. This really happened, but the interesting thing was that it was not reported in the news for two years, in 2014. Some of us would like to believe that this event was just a fluke and is not likely to occur again for a thousand years. Please believe me: it could happen again tomorrow. It is not if, but when. Back in 1869, we were hit. It was known as "the Carrington Event." However, we did not suffer much damage due to not having electrical wires everywhere, nor any electronics. We had what some call the Victorian internet, the telegraph. It burned some telegraph wires and shacks containing the implements needed. Today, just walk outside and look up. We have electrical and telephone wires on poles everywhere. Every part of our lives is run on electronics. We have set ourselves up for disaster and annihilation. Perhaps the worst possibility has to do with nuclear power plants. If we lose power, we cannot cool these reactors indefinitely. Every day, we hear of solar flares, the poles of the earth shifting. David Adair has been pressing Congress to pass a bill that would pay to construct an "Earth Shield." This would protect all of us, but it has now been blocked twice by the same female senator. He said her reasons are all political, but of a personal nature. Who is this woman, and who gave her this kind of power? We could be protected for a few billion dollars—about the amount we send to Pakistan every year. David described what will occur in the first hour when we are hit. It takes a lot to scare me, but I tell you this was more than a little upsetting. A CME event would not only destroy us but also produce a horror on Earth worse than any hell we can imagine. We must press our elected officials to enact the bill to pay for the shield.

I am a firm believer in the Bible. Most of us do not like talking, or hearing, of the end-times. Why? Because it scares us. Every symptom of the end-times is around us, everywhere we look. It has been said by many that it is as though we are following a script. The fact that every prophecy in the Bible has come true makes it even more alarming. The Holocaust and the formation of Israel in 1948 were prophesized over two thousand years ago. The apocalypse is to happen in the Middle East. Just look at what is happening there now. It is in the news almost every day.

Scientists and many researchers have discovered that the earth has cycles. They say the earth has suffered many catastrophic events in its history. I at least know of one of these, which was the great flood. Most life on earth was destroyed. The land mass changed dramatically. We have stories of Atlantis and the Moo civilization in the Pacific. They are now all under water. These cycles occur every twelve thousand to fifteen thousand years. We are at the end of the cycle we have been living in. This has been prophesied by many cultures. The Indigenous peoples of the world have long accepted this as fact.

I could easily write this entire book just on this subject. However, I am committed to focusing on things I can do something about. First and foremost, I want to make sure I am personally prepared. Second, I want to do everything I can to help others to be ready. This book is about humanity awakening spiritually and expanding our consciousness. Like millions of others worldwide, I am convinced we are running out of time. Awakening for each of us must begin by turning our attention within. I will go much deeper on this subject later in this book.

When we fully understand the true meaning of our existence, only then do we discover we have nothing to fear. We learn that we are all eternal. When I think of the end-times, and that we should have died in 2012, it makes me think of all the things I have worried about and realize that none of it matters. I look at the chaos in the world, the wars, and think how utterly silly it all seems. In the end, the only thing that matters is love, how we have treated each other in our lives here. This is all we can take with us.

Most researchers now say that December 21, 2012, marked the beginning of the shift. There is little doubt that from that point, the solar activity has increased significantly. The poles of the earth began shifting. Most importantly, people have been awakening by the thousands every day.

# 3

## MY SPIRITUAL JOURNEY

I want to share my spiritual journey and teach others what I have learned in my lifetime. I have often thought, "I wish I knew then what I know now." I now understand the learning process was all part of the purpose of my existence. The pain, suffering, and challenges are placed in our lives to help us grow and evolve. My spiritual journey began earlier in my life than most people. If you want the details, read my book *Shining Bear*. It was so painful writing that story once, I do not dare do it again. However, for those readers who have not read that book, I will give you the CliffsNotes here.

When I was a young man in my early thirties, people said I had it all. I was well educated, had a very successful career, a wonderful wife, home, cars, money, etcetera. Then I lost both my parents only eight months apart. I had been very close to them and was devastated. Before I had grieved their loss, my wife was diagnosed with cancer at age twenty-nine. She died a slow and painful death less than two years later, at age thirty-one. However, six months earlier, when we learned she was terminal, my only brother suddenly died of a massive heart attack. My wife and I had been together since college, all our adult life. I later learned that I had gone into shock for a year. I was not only devastated but also suicidal. I turned to alcohol and came close to destroying myself. Because of my drinking, I made some bad choices. I lost everything I had, and I do mean everything. I could see no way forward. I wanted to die but did not have the courage to kill myself. After a couple of years, some friends got me into a recovery center for alcoholism. It took a few attempts, but I finally took my last drink in August of 1987. This marked the point where my spiritual journey began. I completely surrendered and completely let go of all control. Let go and let God!

One of the first questions I was asked by a psychologist was, "Harry, what is it that you want?" Then she said nothing. We sat there in silence as I pondered her question. I finally answered and said, "I just want to be happy." I find myself getting emotional even now. I had been unhappy for so very long. I felt completely alone in the world. She next asked me what would it take to make me happy. I honestly did not know. I told her I wanted to get back into my career and get my money back. She replied that she understood but pointed out that true happiness comes from within, not outside ourselves. So she began giving me a plan on how to rebuild my life from the inside out. She said the career and money would come later but would mean nothing unless I found happiness within my own heart and soul. It is important to note that at that point, I had nothing left to lose. There is a lot of freedom in that. I do not know how, but I understood what was being suggested. I also had to sign a contract stating that I would do everything they asked of me. Even now, this fact informs me of how low I was because otherwise, there is no way I would have agreed to sign that agreement. Still, I am sure glad I did. arryH

The process began by getting me into the habit of always looking within, regardless of the situation. We are powerless over people, places, and things. The only control we really possess is over our own choices and actions. At the same time, I had the practice of self-honesty drilled into me daily. Without honesty, there is little to no value to looking within. For example, if I encountered someone that annoyed me, or someone I just did not like, I had to first look within and ask myself why. I have no power over this person, only over myself. Sometimes, I discovered that I saw a character flaw in this person that I knew subconsciously existed within me. This is called mirror imaging, seeing yourself in others. We cannot fix a problem, such as a character flaw, until we first identify it. So instead of bitching about the other person, it helped me to identify my own issues and grow in character. Other times, I would discover the person who got on my nerves had problems I was unaware of. When I learned of their challenges, I could empathize and try to help them. I soon began to realize how we are all connected, not so different, and much the same. Although my recovery involved a lot more work and detail, this was the foundation. The whole concept was about producing a spiritual awakening. This had occurred within me, and it felt great. I wanted more and more. I would spend the next decades seeking enlightenment, studying all things spiritual. All the intense personal work I did, and continue to do, has given me the true happiness and inner peace I had longed for. However, it did not lift the obsession to drink alcohol from me. No human power could have done that. This occurred when I went before almighty God, on my knees, and said, "God, either help me or let me die." I meant it, and God knew I did. Following that moment, my life began to change. I cannot explain it, but it was one little coincidence after another. All I know is soon thereafter, I never again had a desire to take another drink.

After a year of working on myself nonstop twenty-four hours a day, I finally returned to my professional career. I built a business, which became successful. I met my wife Maggie, my soulmate, at the same time. Things were happening in my life that I could take no credit for, including my business. Maggie and I both know that our marriage came about only through divine intervention. There are no accidents in God's world. When we were married, at the Cathedral of Saint Philip in Atlanta, we were truly bonded in holy matrimony. There are two bodies but one spirit. We began our lives together, walking hand and hand, down a spiritual path. We are just celebrating thirty-five years of marriage. Over the years, as we have grown spiritually, our love has only gotten deeper and deeper.

A few years earlier, before I had entered a recovery program, I had attended a seminar on the Silva method of mind control. Although I was still drinking at the time, I never forgot it. It had left a huge impact on me. So Maggie and I took the basic lecture series again, her first time and my second. Later, I continued and took the advanced course with the late José Silva himself. The core of the mind control method is controlling your own mind, thoughts, and using creative imagination to create your own reality. It begins with the use of precise meditation techniques to slow brain wave activity down to the alpha level. This is the creative level. Children are walking around in alpha, which is why they are sponging up everything and quickly. This is also where our basic programming for life occurs. Psychologists tell us that children already have their basic morals and values instilled by an early age, four to eight years. We can also reprogram ourselves by going into the alpha state. Even the first time I was exposed to these techniques and tried them, I was blown away. Although I only had a basic understanding of how it worked then, I have since gained a much deeper understanding, through quantum physics. Basically, it is simple: everything we see in the physical world—a chair, a table, ourselves—is only electromagnetic energy, vibrating at a certain frequency. Words and thought move energy and energy changes matter. In 1924, Dr. Albert Einstein published his theory of relativity. With this, he proved what I just said, that everything, including us, is just energy. Furthermore, he proved that energy can never be destroyed, only transformed. I used these techniques to build my business, opening regional offices all over the country. Within a few years, I had gotten my money back, had a large and beautiful home, and was driving a new 5 series BMW. I had also joined a gym, hired a personal trainer, and was dedicated to my personal fitness. We attended church every Sunday, and I continued my twelve-step meetings. At night, I began reading everything spiritual I could get my hands on. I was reading two books per week for several years. One of these books was *The Celestine Prophecy*. It was a fictional book, and the setting was in Peru. I loved the book, but it had triggered something deep inside me. Suddenly, I had this strong inner need to go to Peru. Everyone thought I was crazy, including me. No one would go with me, so I finally went alone. I had planned the trip very well. I had two guides waiting for me upon arrival in Cusco. I wrote in depth about my experiences in *Shining Bear*.

I did not disclose everything, though. I knew something was pulling me to go there, like a magnet. Once there, the people reacted to me in ways that shocked my guides. It was as though they knew me, and I knew them. Then I spent a couple of days at Machu Picchu. I was spending the nights at this tiny hotel that was just outside the entry gate to the citadel of Machu Picchu. Late one afternoon, after all the tourists had left and they closed, I was allowed to enter alone. There is a large grassy area below, where the leader of the Inca might address his people. I was lying on my back in a deep meditation. I began having intense visions of the people who had inhabited the citadel long ago. I did write about a piece of this, but here is what I did not disclose. A voice came to me and said, "You were Manco Capac." At the time, the name meant nothing to me. I later learned he was the first ruler of the Inca Empire. A few days later, I was riding in the back seat of a car, and that same voice came into my head and again said, "You were Manco Capac." I rejected it, saying, "No way." The reply came back, saying, "Yes, you were." I honestly did not know what to make of it. I did know there had been a force pulling me to go there. I also knew the reaction of the people to me appeared very unusual, and I felt like I had been there before.

# 4

## A NEW PATH APPEARS

During this time, I read a couple of books by Dr. Alberto Villoldo. While working on his thesis for his PhD, he was researching the spiritual teachings and practices of the Indigenous people of the world. So much of this knowledge in the native American culture had been lost, decimated by us whites. However, he had discovered that most of this knowledge remained intact with the Quechua people of Peru. He went there and soon heard the myth of the Quero, who were the spiritual leaders, at the time the Spanish invaded in 1532. I wrote of these people earlier. On my second visit there, I met with Dr. Villoldo. He convinced me to study and train with him. This was the beginning of my "shamanic path," which would continue for several years. I would eventually become a teacher. I had indeed learned a lot about moving energy through my Silva Mind Control practices, but the shamanic path took me to a whole new level. It was during this time that I traveled back into Peru with Alberto and met with the Quero. This had a profound effect on me, one I carry close to me to this day. I also traveled into the Amazon jungle and participated in a couple of Ayahuasca ceremonies.

I experienced many things during those years. I acquired so much knowledge, most of which I wrote about in my last book. There were a few things that became building blocks that took me to another level. One of these was the knowledge that we are all just energy, vibrating at our own frequency. This would become a key foundational learning block to advance my spiritual growth. Next, I learned about emotions. We live in a world of duality. For energy to flow, there must be a positive and a negative charge. For everything there is a polar opposite. There are two basic emotions: love and fear. Yes, there many variations of each. God gave us free will. Every day is a new beginning, and we can choose to come from within ourselves from a place of love, or from a place of fear. Love manifests in many wonderful ways; happiness, joy, empathy, compassion, inner peace. Fear manifest itself in many ways in contrast to love; anger is fear turned outward. Depression is fear turned inward. Then we have hatred, rage, violence, jealousy, envy, and a huge one called greed. In some people, fear manifests as being power crazy. I have worked very hard to choose to come from within myself from love. However, the truth is we all have both light and dark within us. On any given day, I can find some of both within myself. In addition, many say there are some good fears. I cannot disagree with that, at least not in the 3D reality we have existed in. Perhaps the most important truths I have learned are the following: "fear" is our enemy and prevents us from ascending, and our true purpose in life is to learn love, for ourselves and for everyone else.

I also learned the critical nature of honesty, particularly self-honesty. I had this pounded into me by my parents and teachers, and in recovery. I had believed myself to be honest. I soon learned the fallacy of that belief. The biggest lies we tell are those we tell to ourselves. Even worse are the secrets we keep from ourselves. Later in this book, I will talk about the secret of all secrets we have all lived with. It has to do with who we are. For me, I started down this path by examining my emotions, my feelings toward others. I am not even responsible for what you think of me. What matters is how I "honestly" think of myself. This means if I cannot go to the Lord in prayer with a clear conscience, I am in trouble. Deep down, we all know whether we have a clean conscience. I think this is a major reason people turn away from God. We intuitively know that before God, there are no secrets. We are compelled to face the truth about ourselves. I still make mistakes and always will. I have screwed up so many times in my life that I cannot count. There are two differences in how I deal with my mistakes today, in comparison to how I dealt with them before. First, I always examine what occurred and why. Then, I learn from it and do my best never to repeat it. Yet I have done that too. I can only hope God has a sense of humor. Secondly, I immediately admit my part in the mistake, offer my apologies to the other person, and be willing to do what is required to make restitution when necessary. Then I go directly to the Lord, admit my mistake, and ask forgiveness. This keeps my conscience clean and clear.

As I have revealed before, I studied the spiritual and healing practices of the ancient Inca, the Quechua people, for several years. Initially, I was learning and trying to absorb so much, I did not have enough time to process it all. I was still building and running my business at the time. What amazes me to this day is how similar their spiritual practices are, to Christianity and other major religions of the world. In *Shining Bear*, I often spoke of the necessity for us to practice what I call "universal truths." This is so simple, and I find it sad that people fight and kill one another over un-important differences. The simple fact is this: truth is truth, regardless of where we hear it from. Secondly, it is about what is in our hearts, not in our heads, that truly matter. I am, and have always been, a Christian, trying to follow the teachings of Jesus Christ. When I met with the Quero, they had never heard of Jesus. However, as oweverHI listened to what they believed and how they lived, I realized what they described was closer to the teachings of Christ than what I have witnessed in Christian churches. For example, they were all about love, pure love. If there is one teaching taught by Jesus that no one can argue or debate, it is the practice of nonjudgment. Jesus shocked many of his own disciples when he turned to help sinners, like prostitutes and tax collectors. I have personally witnessed many Christian churches not only pass judgment on "sinners," but also throw them out. One of the first practices I was taught on this shamanic path was that of nonjudgment. It was not just about judging other people but anything, any situation, as good or bad. Initially, I recall thinking this would be easy for me, as I did not consider myself very judgmental. Again, I was in for a shock. We were to focus on this practice for six months. When I returned for the next direction of the medicine wheel, Alberto asked me how I did. I was embarrassed to have to tell him I felt a failure. I had no idea just how judgmental I was. Yes, I judged others, but more than that, I judged everything. I was surprised when he smiled at me, saying, "Harry, you are on the right path." Before we can resolve a flaw in character, we must first recognize it. I had certainly succeeded in that aspect. I soon realized nonjudgment was much like getting honest with myself. It would require a lifetime of persistent work and focus to change and grow. I am still guilty of some judgment, as well as dishonesty with myself. I know I will never be perfect, but it is more about progress than perfection. I learned to only compare myself with myself. When I look at where I am today compared to when I began, I am utterly amazed. It is so easy to judge others, but looking into a mirror requires guts and a lifelong commitment.

# 5

## FACING MY FEAR OF DEATH

Before my wife Kathy died, she told me that if there was a way, she would contact me after she crossed over. She was much better prepared for this than I was. She did contact me, several times. There were witnesses to a few of these contacts. Following her death, someone gave me a book entitled *Life after Life*, by Dr. Raymond Moody. The book had been published in 1975, and was a groundbreaker. He had studied many case histories of people who had near-death experiences, called NDEs. His book was the first, but since that time, there have been so many books and documentaries on this subject. At the time, I was not sure what to believe, but it sure was comforting. When Kathy began contacting me, I became a believer. For years, people who had had NDEs did not talk about them or quickly learned not to discuss them. Some had told their doctors and were placed in psychiatric wards. Their own spouses and families ridiculed them. Yet these experiences had a profound effect on each one, which lasted for a lifetime. After I lost my wife and my entire family, a question arose within me, one that humans have been asking throughout history: Is there life after life, or when you are dead, is that truly the end? Religions have told us we live on, in the spirit world. Science had told us we are just matter, meaning dust to dust and ashes to ashes. When you die, you are dead. This has changed, and we now have a science that appears to agree with religion. This is quantum physics. It is important to know that although we only began hearing of them some fifty years ago, this is nothing new. Hippocrates, the ancient Greek physician, who is considered the most important figure in the history of medicine, wrote about NDEs. The Romans wrote stories about this phenomenon. They provide us with the best proof we have that the death of the body is not the end of life. I will go into this much deeper later in this book.

The biggest fear most humans have is death. It is fear of the unknown. If we can overcome that fear, we are truly free to live our lives. I was taught, while on the shamanic path, that when we go to the west direction of the medicine wheel, we must die to our old selves and travel over the rainbow bridge into the world beyond. This is where the Ayahuasca came into play. I did participate, but it was not a snap decision. I had never thought I would consider doing this. I trained for at least five years. I just had to know. I wrote about this experience in *Shining Bear*. There had been very few people in my life that had known of this part of my journey. My wife knew, and those I had traveled into Peru with knew, but that was it. In the first draft of my manuscript, I had created an illusion to cover up this part of my story. However, it felt so bad inside me that I went back and told it the way it was. I knew some readers would have objections to the choices I had made, and a few did. The question at the time for me was: How do you fully explain this to people with no foundation of knowledge on the subject? I then realized my error; I was worrying about what others would think, which I have no control over. Besides, one of the biggest and most profound teachings I had received on my last journey was the critical necessity for self-honesty. *Shining Bear* has been extremely well received, and only ones or two people took issue, and only a couple even mentioned it. For the most part, my readers were able to look beyond and see how these experiences had benefited me and helped me to evolve. During the ceremony, I was out of my body for several hours. I met my maternal grandfather, who had died prior to my birth. He showed me "videos" of me as a child and how he had been with me. This confirmed for me that there is indeed life after death of the body. While out of my body, I could go anywhere, visit any person, and do so instantaneously. The most important thing I was shown was the quantum field, that everyone and everything in our reality is connected. In physics today, they have what is called "string theory." The stings are the smallest part of the atom, if I understand it correctly. I could not only see these strings while out of body but could also trace them. In our 3D reality, we now know that we, humanity, create the world around us. It begins with the thought. Thought moves energy, and energy changes matter. I would have a thought, literally see the energy produced, and then track that energy to see the impact on whomever or whatever I had thought of. This is where I began to see the necessity for rigorous honesty. Perhaps more important was the need for positive thinking. If we think negative thoughts about someone, we are literally doing that person harm, even if you have never met the person in question. In contrast to this, if we send positive thoughts and love to a person, we are helping them. It is simple to say these words, but during my experience, I was able to literally see these waves of energy impact the target of my thought. At the time, I had no idea that science, through quantum mechanics, had proven these very things. Quantum mechanics has proven that when we look at someone or something, it is changed. The "observer" changes reality.

When the experience ended at daylight the next morning, I kept saying to my friends; "I just cannot believe it; it is so darn simple." My friend asked me what was so simple. I replied, "Life is so simple." Today, I tell you this is still true. The problem is inside us. We complicate life for ourselves and for everyone around us. This is because of fear. In the next chapter, I will expand on this subject. I recall my departure from the jungle. It took two days for me to get home. I knew when I left that I would never be the same person I had been before. I thought about every aspect of the journey, out of body, all the way home. It took several years for me to fully process it. I am still processing it to some degree. What it did was build a foundation of a new understanding of life. I think of it as the beginning, like being in kindergarten, and my spiritual growth continued from there. *Shining Bear* basically took the reader to where I had arrived within myself over twenty years ago. I have evolved so much since then. The experience did have some immediate impact on how I lived my life and interacted with people. For example, I avoid negative people like the plague. I cannot bear to be around negative and angry people. Many people have read my book and surmised this was a near-death experience. It was not, but there are a few similarities. For instance, I had listened to many people who have had NDEs. No matter how educated, articulate, and descriptive they may be, all say there is just no words to describe what they experienced. So whom do they discuss their experience with, especially when there are so many who refuse to believe any part of it? In my case, I had much the same problem. I later learned the ayahuasca experiences are different for each person. It comes down to the "intent" of each who participate. I had indeed received everything I intended and more. I got what I needed. I have been told that each person who has an NDE is shown exactly what they need to see. I see the NDE as being God ordained. Those people did not choose to have the experience. I had made the choice. I must tell you that I was full of fear. It took every ounce of courage I could muster. Ayahuasca is often called "the Rope of Death." This is because the participant must face their own death, face all their fears. I do not recommend anyone do this. I was well prepared and had received a vast amount of training over several years. In the final analysis, because I faced my deepest fears, I found a new freedom unlike any I had ever known. It expanded my mind and has allowed me to understand so much about who we are, in truth. In my shamanic training, I had been told I needed to discover the secret we all keep from ourselves. No one would tell me what that secret was. I had to find out for myself. I had received the answer in the jungle, but it would take several more years before I could connect the dots.

I am now convinced that we are here to evolve spiritually, in consciousness, and to learn how to love. Throughout our lives, we are given opportunities to help us to accomplish this feat. We all have free will. I had followed my heart, which led me on the path that ended in the Amazon. I could have easily allowed fear to alter my path. I am grateful that God was always with me, helping me to find the courage to seek truth and the answers I sought. I would like you, the reader, to understand that what I have shared thus far was not the end of my quest, but the beginning. In the next chapter, you will learn where the foundational teaching took me.

# 6

## KNOW THYSELF

In Delphi at the temple of Apollo, there is an inscription at the top of the arch that reads, "Know Thyself." This is from ancient Greece, long before the time of Jesus. However, the Bible also tells us the same thing: know thyself. Many historians and theologians have discovered the ancients were far more advanced spiritually than the population of the world today. I have heard it said many times, from multiple sources, that humans are a species with amnesia. We have forgotten who we are. Today, I have arrived at the same conclusion.

I have shared before how, forty years ago, I lost everything I had. When I began rebuilding my life from the inside out, I came to understand that all I wanted, had ever wanted, was to be happy. As the years passed, I came to realize this is truly what we all want. Since that time, I have spent my life searching for inner peace, joy, and happiness. I finally came to realize I would never find this in the material world. I was terribly slow to catch onto this fact. Along the way, I had many accomplishments; Maggie and I had obtained beautiful homes and cars. Initially, these things always made us happy, but the new wore off each one, faster and faster. We moved across country, from Atlanta to the Phoenix area. Here again, we initially loved it. I enjoyed the dry climate of the desert. I spent a lot of time in Sedona, which was great for meditation. Both of us had received several physical benefits from the dry climate. Here again, the new soon wore off. We both came to realize something was missing. We identified it as just not feeling at home. Both of us had grown up on the East Coast. Our families and our roots were there. We had been married in Atlanta and had many friends there. Although this was all true, I would eventually arrive at the conclusion that the feelings we experienced, of not feeling at home and that something was missing, went much deeper. Intellectually, I knew that our happiness had very little to do with our physical location. For many years, I had believed that my happiness was in proportion to my relationship to God. I still believe this today, but my view of this relationship has shifted. After twelve years living in Arizona, we moved back to Atlanta. Again, we were very happy for a while, but the new wore off again. I need to make something clear before continuing. When I described the feeling that

something was missing, the feeling of never being satisfied, please understand that we were never miserable.
In fact, most everything in our lives was great, especially on the outside. If you have ever awakened on a
given morning and had a feeling of being down, a blue
feeling, but nothing was wrong, this describes how we
felt. The fact is, we have all experienced days like this
I had usually just written these days off as part of life.
For many years, I had traveled all over the country and
outside it. We had gone to London, Paris, and Mexico,
and I had spent a lot of time in South America. I was
continuously seeking spiritual enlightenment. I experienced periods of great inner peace and joy. I just could
not hang onto it very long, especially when I stepped
back into the world of chaos. I sat alone one day in
quiet, reflecting on my life. I had spent my life chasing
one thing or another. I would always think, "When I get
this, I will be happy or satisfied." I realized I had either
been running toward pleasure or trying to avoid pain. I
loved my wife, but deep within, I felt alone, cut off from
others. I remembered that I had always felt something
was missing. I could not seem to reach the inner feeling
of being satisfied. I thought I must spend more time
practicing an attitude of gratitude. I did indeed have so
much to be grateful for, all God's blessings. I had spent
years peeling back layer after layer of myself, trying to
get to the core of who I am. I truly felt I knew myself as
well as anyone could. I was soon to discover the fallacy
in that belief. I had no idea who I truly was.

# 7

## AWAKENING

Some time ago, I watched a documentary entitled *The Awakening Mind*. As I sat there listening to what they were saying, I was amazed. It was as though they were reading my mind. They described virtually every feeling I just wrote about. There were four or five individuals speaking separately. Each one shared their own journey, which seemed to be in direct parallel to my own. They had chased happiness and avoided pain. Regardless of the level of accomplishment, they had always felt a lack of satisfaction, just as I had experienced. Then they began describing the problem and, more importantly, the solution for us all. The root of our problem stems from the illusion of the mind that we are our bodies. The truth is that we are not who we think we are. As I had described the years I spent searching for spiritual enlightenment, I was being told that what we essentially are is already fully awake. We already are love, happiness, and joy. Awakening is the recognition of the true nature of our being. This is much closer to who we are than what we think we are. Earlier, I spoke of the secret we keep from ourselves. This is that secret! I honestly believe that awakening is the answer to virtually all the world's problems. This delusion of the mind is what manifests the feelings of being alone, that we are just our limited egoic selves. It gives us the sense of "It is me against the world." It instills within us the constant battle between fear and love. Most of us live in a state of fear, to varying degrees. The fear is manifesting as hate, anger, greed, violence, envy, jealousy, and crime. The list goes on and on. Once we awaken to who we truly are, all the fear begins to vanish. We are consciousness, individuations of God, and all the same. We then realize we are not limited, that we are creators of our own realities. I had already learned, the hard way, that I could not find happiness through the acquisition of wealth or material possessions. One of the participants of this documentary was Neal Donald Walsh, a very well-known author and speaker. He described precisely what I had experienced in life. He, too, had awakened one day to discover that nothing he had done or accomplished in his life really mattered. They were aspects of life. I am not suggesting that what we do is unimportant. They just are not the point of life. So what is the point? Why am I here? I am here to recognize my true self, to evolve in consciousness, and to learn the art of love. When we recognize who we are, that we are spiritual beings, having a physical experience, we grow up. For me, I could finally understand the true meaning of loving thy neighbor as thyself. My neighbor is myself. We are all consciousness of light and of love. We are all woven together, like in a net. The illusion is in our perception of the physical differences. The ancients knew this. The Buddha said that reality is an illusion. Today, quantum physicists are telling us we are living in a virtual reality. Initially I was very confused in my attempt to understand this. Like many others, I thought this meant our life in this 3D world was not real. Then I learned this is not what it means. It is real, and everything we do matters very much. This is because our choices determine whether we evolve. If we fail to evolve, we then devolve. Eventually, we devolve into nothing. The physical world we experience with our five senses is a virtual reality, created by universal consciousness. I have never played a virtual reality game, but I am told there are some similarities. The player puts on a headset and becomes part of the game, through an avatar representing the player of the game. The game seems very real. However, the consciousness that is making the choices inside the virtual reality is outside the game. We are that consciousness making choices outside the virtual reality of life. I hope this analogy makes sense. I got it by listening to Tom Campbell, a theoretical physicist, who has researched consciousness for forty years. The bottom line here is that we are not who we have believed ourselves to be. We must awaken. This means we must cease to identify ourselves as our bodies, as our limited selves. The truth I have discovered is that we are so much more than what we have been led to believe through years of conditioning. We know our bodies die, but today most of us realize this is not the end, that we live on, and on, and on.

I knew this all rang true. All the problems I had struggled with throughout my life were not unique to me. They were all issues related to living in the 3D reality, a reality of the physical. This is exactly why we see all the chaos in the world today. They are all characteristics of the third density of reality, the third harmonic frequency. Until we evolve into the fourth harmonic frequency, this chaos will continue. Millions of us have made this leap already. More and more people are awakening daily. We are not our bodies. We are consciousness, spiritual beings. This is a huge part of the current "shift" I continue to refer to. Only now did I fully connect the dots from the Ayahuasca journey I had taken to the truth I was now learning. It all made sense. I had experienced the conscious field and literally saw the power of the human mind. I then realized we are so much more and possess unlimited power when we recognize the truth of who we are. We must awaken now. Everyone agrees the world is in chaos and that we cannot continue the path we have been traveling.

# 8

## SCIENCE AND RELIGION
## JOIN AGAIN

I am now convinced that one of the most positive steps toward our awakening has been the reconnection of science and religion. For years, scientist have followed Newtonian physics. The mere mention of anything religious or spiritual would turn them away. In the decade between 1915 and 1925, a revolution in science took place. Einstein had developed his theory of relativity. Then the field of quantum mechanics came into being and continues to evolve to this day. What is quantum physics? I have an elementary understanding but will try and explain. First, we know the atom is the building block of all matter. Inside the atom, we have electrons, protons, and neutrons. When we remove all three of them, we are left with the nucleus. When we split the nucleus, that is nuclear. When the atom bomb was developed, they said we had learned how to split the atom. Quantum means small, and quanta is electromagnetic energy. This is where quantum physics begins, and Newtonian physicists leave the room. Once the atom is split, they found quartz. When they split the quartz, they found strings. This is where the "string theory" comes from. Years ago, when I had my out-of-body experience in the jungle, I saw strings that I could follow. At the time, I had no understanding of the quantum field. I only knew what I had experienced. I feel the need to explain this to make it easier to understand consciousness.

Quantum Mechanics came about during the same time. It was the result of what they referred to as "the double slit experiment." It has to do with the observation of waves of light versus particles. These particles, or photons of light, were passed through double slits. When the waves were passed through, they saw the refraction patterns hit the wall behind it, as they expected. Then they sent photons through, and to their amazement, they saw the same fractal patterns they saw with the wave. This should not have happened. Then to learn and visualize what was occurring, they set up a way to directly observe the photons when they passed through the slits. When they observed the particles, they behaved just as the expected and piled up in a row in front of the slit. Now you may ask why this is a big deal, or even why I am relating this here. We, humanity, are energy, light. Do you remember when I spoke of thinking positive thoughts in the jungle and tracing the strings to the person, seeing the positive impact? What quantum mechanics proved for me was that when we "observe" a person, or think of someone, we change them. How we change someone, or something, by observing, depends on a set of variables or probabilities. Among them are whether we are thinking positively or negatively, whether we are coming from a place of love or fear. In quantum mechanics, they now say there are no particles of light, only probabilities. We are light, and our consciousness can change reality just by observing a person or a thing.

We must awaken to who we truly are that we are all consciousness, from the same God or source. When we hurt, or harm, each other, we are harming ourselves. Believe me, I know this is difficult to comprehend, but every journey begins with the first step.

# 9

## ASCENSION

Before I go any further, I need to tell you that I am a Christian man. What this means to me is that I do everything I can to practice the teachings of Jesus Christ. To do this, we must follow the teaching within the New Testament. When I first stepped onto my path, I was introduced to the work of Emmett Fox, an early-twentieth-century author and lecturer. To paraphrase he said the following: no one today can understand the New Testament without the spiritual key. He wrote a book called *The Sermon on the Mount*. He essentially broke down each verse and explained the meaning, with the spiritual key. He did the same thing with the Lord's Prayer. His work has helped me so much in my understanding and interpretation of biblical scripture. I highly recommend this book, as I have bought many copies for gifts for family and friends. When I thought about it, it is not surprising that we have so many variations of the Christian church. I grew up in a very small town, and there must have been five or six different versions of the Baptist church, all believing they were right and the others were wrong. We all know the Bible has been interpreted over and over, in every language, for centuries. Many good people have made the same mistakes of interpreting it "literally," without the spiritual key. Many religious researchers have said the same things; at the core of most every religion on earth, you find the same basic truths. Whatever the differences, it certainly is not worth killing each other over. Here again, once we all awaken, we will understand we are all the same, of the same light, and of the same God. In recent times, I have heard people questioning everything. Some say the Crucifixion was a hoax or that Jesus was an extraterrestrial. I suggest these people have not done their homework. Much of the New Testament consist of letters written by the apostles, like Paul. Years ago, there were historians who set out to debunk the accuracy contained in these letters. However, not only did they fail to debunk the accuracy, but they also returned, saying that Paul was a historian of the highest order. It is important to remember that the accounts given within these letters are by those who were either there at the time of Jesus, or immediately afterward, and working with those who were present and traveled with Jesus.

So the question I began asking was this: "What did Jesus really teach?" We know the present Bible was compiled over three hundred years after the Crucifixion. We also know that much was omitted at the Council of Nicene. After the end of WWII, there were two important archeological discoveries; most everyone has heard of the Dead Sea Scrolls. This was in 1947. In the same time frame, the Nag Hammadi texts were discovered in Egypt, in 1945. Both texts interested me in a huge way. The reason is that they exposed the truths practiced by the early Christians. To me, it is only logical that the early Christians knew more about the specific teachings of Jesus than those constructing the Bible three hundred years later. There have always been a few Christian beliefs that never made sense to me. I just never knew why. Each time I tried asking questions, people became angry and defensive. For example, I was never able to grasp the idea that Jesus died this horrific death for our sins. I am not saying this is not true, just that I failed to understand it. Yes, he certainly taught us forgiveness. In the Lord's Prayer, it says, "Forgive us our trespasses as we forgive those who trespass against us." This I get and have done my best to practice. Still, this did not help me to understand why he had to die for my sins. Now in the Nag Hammadi text, we find Jesus saying, "I did not come here to save you but to remind you of who you truly are. That we are light beings, of the Father in heaven." This is what the early Christians practiced and taught.

In fact, it is what many of the ancients taught before the time of Jesus. Much of what is written in the two discovered sets of text we written by a group called the "Essenes," that were active before Jesus began his ministry. John the Baptist was a member, and they were highly evolved in spiritual teachings. They taught of the divine spark within us. Their teachings were prevalent in the Dead Sea Scrolls. People were shocked to discover many of the teachings were almost identical to those of Jesus. An example given was the Sermon on the Mount. It is almost word for word what the Essenes wrote. International speaker David Lorimar talked about the Cathars in southern France, who practiced the Gnostic teachings. The Gnostics wrote most of the Nag Hammadi text. They say that following the Crucifixion of Jesus, Mary Magdelene came there and taught for twenty years. They were taught, and practiced, the same principles: that we have the light of God within us, a divine spark. In those early centuries, the church considered this heresy. The church represented the law, and the Cathars represented the spirit. It almost seems the church did not want anyone to confront the divine directly. Only the church was to have that capacity. So many of these early Christian teachings were suppressed. Furthermore, the Romans killed most of the Essenes in AD 60. The Catholic Church had many of the Gnostics killed. Both the Romans, and later the church, saw them as a threat to their power. However, they would surface several times over the centuries. Professor and author Betty Kovacs teaches that we are now in the fifth renaissance. A few hundred years ago, during a renaissance period, these teachings surfaced in a major way. The people were full of excitement. Many great cathedrals were built in Europe, especially in France. Inside twenty-two of these cathedrals, there was a labyrinth on the floor. A person entered with a question, walked around, and down, until they came to the end. There they confronted the divine, not as other, but as self. We are all individuations of God. Kovacs also spoke of the "grail" story, which we have all heard of. The grail is not a cup. She describes it as the boy goes into the world, has countless experiences, meets many people, and bonds with nature. This is the labyrinth. During this time, he learns more and more about himself. In the end he reaches the deepest part of himself, the soul, which is the holy grail. Here, he confronts the divine. According to Betty, there have been four previous renaissance periods, chances for humanity to awaken, ascend, and evolve. Each time, forces came in that stopped it. This may be our last chance. Today, we have a lot going for us that we never had before. We now have science back on our side, particularly quantum physicists; we have the internet, and the world is much smaller. We have countless ways to spread the word. In the past, we might read about a disaster on the other side of the world, where many lost their lives and thousands were suffering. Today, we can see live video, look into the eyes of the victims, and feel empathy and compassion. This has brought us closer together, helping us to realize we are all one, not separate. Today, there is a new renaissance of awakening to these same Gnostic teachings. Millions of people worldwide are embracing them. What makes them so compelling to me is that they consist of the precise words of the early Christians. The Bible and other religious scriptures have been translated and retranslated so many times that there must be numerous errors. Another critical point is this: the church has taught us the teachings of Jesus, while he was in his flesh-and-blood state, living among us. Following his resurrection, he appeared many times to his disciples, teaching them of the afterlife, and how to navigate it. The Gnostic writings are said to contain the teachings of the "living Christ," meaning Jesus after he ascended. Following the findings of the Dead Sea Scrolls in 1947, they were mostly sequestered for three to four decades. They feared it could topple the church.

I keep asking myself: How did we get so far from these truths? Why were they suppressed again and again? I completely agree with William Henry, an author and mystic investigator. He said the darkest philosophy ever invented was "materialism." This seems to have been started by science, especially by Newtonian physicist. They taught us that everything, including us, is just matter and that consciousness is just an artifact of brain activity. They taught us that we are born, we live a few years, and then die. The end! This filtered down into our schools and education system. This has led many to reject the idea of a God. They believed that religion was for the weak and ignorant. In addition, it has led many of us to allow our ego to be our master. This, in turn, has led to the quest for wealth, power, acquisition of material, and never looking within, only outward. Perhaps even worse, we have become self-centered, continuously seeking pleasure and avoiding pain. I had struggled for years to get my ego out of my way. I now think of ego as the focus on me, me, me. I now spend much of my time thinking of others. I am not suggesting that all ego is bad. It can be a good servant but a horrible master. What has occurred over the years is that by living the philosophy of materialism, we are out of balance, and we are living in disharmony with the earth.

For years I heard psychologist talking about healing our inner child. I really did not understand this, and frankly, it sounded a bit new age for my taste. I now know I was wrong, but mostly uninformed. When I was born, it soon became evident that I was left handed. My parents tried to switch me but soon gave up. At the time, I had no idea why they wanted me to use my right hand. I later learned it had arrived from some superstition posed by the church. I never gave this further thought, until recent years. Besides, I threw a ball right handed and swung a bat and a golf club right handed. I eat and write with my left hand. There are two lobes in our brain. The left brain is associated with logic and reason. The right is where our intuitive nature derives from, our more sensitive nature. Being left handed is indicative of being right brained. But I use both sides. The right lobe is of feminine energy, and the left side is of the masculine energy. For those not so informed, this has nothing to do with sex or gender. We are all just energy, vibrating at a given frequency. This topic only refers to our energy. To become whole, balanced, we must bring both sides of our brain together. This is where the psychologists speak of healing your inner child. We have all been hurt, wounded by others, at some time in our lives. This is where forgiveness becomes so important. When I first got into a recovery program, a twelve-step program, I just did what I was told. I had no idea that I was healing this inner child. In step 8, we made a list of all those we had harmed, in any way. In step 9, we made those amends wherever possible. At the time, all I knew was that it felt great. Today, I thank God I found those steps. I have said many times that the steps have nothing to do with alcoholism, nor did the originate with the founders of the AA program. If every human on earth worked these steps, it would transform life as we know it. The bottom line is that we must evolve in consciousness to enter the kingdom of God. To do this, we must turn our attention inward, to know thyself.

# 10

## NEAR-DEATH EXPERIENCES

Earlier, I mentioned how the advent of quantum physics and the internet are helping us in this evolution of consciousness. There is still another thing we now have NDEs, near-death experiences. We began studying this phenomenon in the midtwentieth century. I spoke of how I lost my family, and finally my wife, in rapid succession many years ago. Someone gave me a book entitled *Life after Life*, by Dr. Raymond Moody. He had studied several dozen cases of NDEs and found countless similarities with each. I can certainly report that I found great comfort in his words. This was nothing new and had been going on for probably from the beginning. However, these experiencers never talked about it. The ones that did were labeled as nuts and sent to psychiatric wards. Some of this behavior persists to this day, but is far less common. The reason is that since Dr. Moody published his book, there have been millions of these cases reported worldwide. Many books have been written, including many by the experiencers themselves. This is where the old scientist, students of Newtonian physics, have come up against impossible facts. When the body dies, the heartbeat flatlines, and so does the EEG, the brain wave activity. According to their science, if there is zero brain activity, the person should not have any experience. However, we have thousands returning from death reporting incredible stories and visuals. I have heard stories of patients dying in the operating room, floating upward on the ceiling before traveling onward. When they were resuscitated, they reported hearing every word spoken, even by nurses, whom they had not seen prior to their surgery. They returned describing specific medical devices, which they previously had no knowledge of and which surgeon used each. How could the naysayers explain this? Others have stated that before their NDE, they were atheist or agnostic. During their experiences they reported encounters with Jesus, or even God, where they were shown and taught many things. When they returned, they were forever changed and became very spiritual people. I read a book by Dr. Eben Alexander, a neurosurgeon, who has an incredible story. He suddenly because extremely ill and was in a coma for several days. His central nervous system was filled with a nasty bacterium. The doctors told his family he was unlikely to live and that even if he did, he would be brain dead. Not only did he live and regained full function but also reported an incredible and beautiful story in vivid detail. Most all the experiencers reported going through a life review. I had heard of the Akashic records for years. Today, quantum physicists claim to have proven the existence of what they call a database, which contains a record of everything we say or do in this life, but also all our past lives, whether we have lived twenty or twenty thousand lives. I know that reincarnation is a sensitive subject among many of my Christian brothers and sisters. Yet many experiencers of NDEs have reported being shown several past lives. Perhaps this may sound crazy to some, but I have always had this deep knowing that I have lived before. My wife Maggie has had the same feelings. When I had my out-of-body experience in the Amazon jungle and met with the spirits and angels, I was told that I was an "old soul," having lived many lives. Most all the ancients believed this, and Eastern religions believe it to this day. In addition, every scientist in the field of quantum physics has confirmed this as fact. Several years ago, there was a researcher at the University of Virginia who was a nonbeliever in reincarnation. His name was Dr. Ian Stevenson. He set out to prove his point. After much research, following many in-person interviews, with mostly children and their parents, he not only failed in proving that reincarnation did not exist but also became a staunch believer. I have personally read about some of his cases and watched documentaries. The facts are undeniable. There are simply no other explanations other than the fact these individuals had indeed lived past lives. Today, the practice of past-life regression has become an industry worldwide. I admit, I have arrived at the conclusion this is truth. Furthermore, it explains so many questions I have previously been unable to answer. It ties so many things together. To learn the art of love, to love our neighbor as ourselves, takes a lot of time. Each life we live moves us a little further, until we get it right. I cannot prove this, but most spiritual beliefs held by people cannot be objectively proven. I have learned to trust my gut instincts, the little voice inside me. I think of this little voice as the God within me. It has never been wrong. I now understand this is my inner consciousness, which is netted with all consciousness in the universe. Several years ago, I got this idea that I was not learning anything but remembering. Initially, I thought this must be insane, my imagination gone wild. Today, I believe there was truth in that idea. I heard a woman who had had an NDE say the same thing. Now I understand the reason for this. As consciousness, we have access to all information in the universe.

# 11

## THE EARLY CHRISTIAN

The Essenes and the Cathars referred to themselves as the "Perfecti," or the perfect ones This did not mean they believed they were perfect as people but balanced. Awakening means to remember who we truly are. What we essentially are is already our higher self, spirit, consciousness, and love. We have all been caught up in the illusion that we are just physical, that we are our bodies. The body is important as it is the temple of the soul. The 3D reality is a physical reality. When we begin to awaken to who we truly are, we begin moving away from fear and toward love. Our vibration increases until we enter the fourth harmonic frequency. Simply put, this is the evolution I am talking about. This is the purpose of our lives here, to evolve, and learn how to love, not fear. When we arrive at the realization that we are eternal, that there is no death, we automatically drop a large amount of our fear. My extensive study of NDEs has proven to me that life is eternal, that the death of our body is not the death we all fear. Quantum physicists now say that consciousness is fundamental in the universe. However, they also say that time and space are not fundamental. We live our lives on a linear calendar. As we evolve, our sense of time will also change. I have no intention of getting into temporal dynamics here. This is so far above my head, but I mention it because it is important to know that time is not what we have believed it to be. It is not linear, and as we move into the fourth and fifth density, we will begin to grasp this. For example, time travel is possible, and I have heard some humans are doing it now. This is another example of why we must expand our mind and consciousness. Nothing in God's world is impossible. Anything we can imagine can be created. Maintaining an open mind is critical. Please do not allow yourself to become trapped by practicing the concept of "contempt prior to investigation," which guarantees a life of perpetual ignorance.

When we look around at what is happening in the world today, there is so much evil, depression, suicide, and drug addiction. This is because so many people have removed God from the equation. A couple of years ago, I had fallen into watching documentaries on serial killers. Magie asked me why I was watching this morbid stuff. I was trying to understand the how, and the why. One of the documentaries, a British one, went into the background of these killers. I still do not have all the answers, but there was one constant in virtually every case; none had ever had God in their lives. There was no evidence of anything spiritual in any part of their lives. Religions have told us that no one can enter heaven without having been tested by the devil. In the New Testament, we have Jesus going out into the wilderness for forty days and nights, where he was tested by the devil. Professor Ravi Revendra poses the question for everyone to ask themselves: How many millions of dollars would it take for you to betray something or someone? As for myself, today there is no amount of money large enough to get me to betray anyone or any principal. One the other hand, I hate to admit it, but there were several years in my life when I could not say this. I know today that the life we live in our bodies is temporary and was never intended to be permanent. I know I have a purpose here, and the idea of betraying something is betraying myself. I do not want to have to keep doing this over and over, in more incarnations. I want to live in paradise with Jesus and our Father.

Ascension is about the transformation from a fear-based frequency to a love-based one. We do not need to go anywhere, nor do anything, for this to occur. It is a pathless path. We must be quiet and not allow our mind to control us, just be. Getting my mind out of the way has always been my biggest challenge. So I practice the old concept of "Fake it until you make it." I go into a meditative state, telling myself I am not my body, that I am spirit. I then project myself outside my physical body and into my light body. I then bond with Jesus and can travel anywhere instantly. In the past few months, I have had two relatives in serious physical condition. I have gone to them, along with Jesus, and performed energetic healing work. One was in a coma and the other in congestive heart failure. After I worked on each for two days, both miraculously recovered. They happened a few months apart and on different sides of the country. Perhaps it was just a coincidence, but I do not believe in coincidences. I have had similar things happen for many years. I never take credit. I have always given credit to God. We are all just energy, light, from the same God. Today, medical researchers have designed many healing tools based entirely on frequency and energy. This is indeed the future of medicine and healing.

My true concern is that we are running out of time. Either we awaken, become fully aware, and expand our consciousness, or most believe it will be the end of humanity on earth. The sad thing is that this is so simple. It differs from the narrative we have all embraced. If we want things to change, we must embrace this new paradigm. If we can just get everyone to practice the Golden Rule, life on earth would be transformed overnight. The Golden Rule tells us to do unto others as we would have them do unto us. When we awaken to the fact our neighbor is ourself, hurting him only hurts ourself. Another way to look at the Golden Rule is that we get back exactly what we put out. If you do not like what life is giving you, then look at what you are putting out. Practicing the Golden Rule does not mean you must become religious. It is a "universal law" that has been around for all time. When I was a kid, I would break rules and try to get away with them. Although my parents always seemed to find out, I now know that I never got away with anything. When we send out negative energy, it always comes back to us, in one form or another. People talk about karma, which I believe in. Some say it transfers from one life to another. I do not know whether there is truth in that or not. I do know what we send out comes back every time. This is because it is all energy, which has no ending. It may return in ways we never expected and many years later. I know that even if I did something that no one knew about, there is always at least one person on earth that knows. That person is *me*. God also knows. Plus, everything we do, every choice we make, is recorded in the Akashic record for all time. There is an old saying: "Your secrets will keep you sick." I have lived long enough to know this is a true statement. I have seen secrets destroy people; one was a good friend of mine. He failed to get honest with himself. We must face our worst fears and confront all our secrets. Failure to do this has terrible consequences and will destroy your quality of life. There really are no big deals.

# 12

## MORE ABOUT THE ESSENES AND THE GNOSTICS

The Gnostic teachings are going through a global renaissance today. To me, the most compelling reason to take this work seriously is because it comes directly from the earliest Christian teachings, by those who lived with and traveled with Jesus. The words are "straight from the horse's mouth," to use the phrase. Before I could take them to heart, I first needed to know who these people were.

About three hundred years before Jesus, many mystics, scholars, and religious missionaries met at the great library of Alexandria in Egypt. They were Buddhist from India, Hindus, Hebrews from Palestine, and philosophers from Greece. They came together to discuss human transformation and ascension. The

Greeks believed that our souls are prisoners of the human body. They wanted to find a way to escape the process of having to be reincarnated over and over. So they discussed this and ways to ascend back into our celestial form. They believed that Adam and Eve, in the Garden of Eden, were originally in their celestial form, without physical bodies. Then the serpent appears, they eat from the forbidden fruit, gain the knowledge of good and evil, and the punishment was they were placed into physical bodies. They also believed this was the beginning of the creation of the simulation, the virtual reality, or holographic universe we are now being told we live in. The Buddha is known to have said the reality we live in is an illusion. This began the search to discover methods to evolve back into our celestial, or light bodies. In Tibet, they speak of attaining your "rainbow body." I confess this sounded far-fetched to me. However, most every person who has experienced an NDE, has reported they did not want to come back. In addition, there have been tens of thousands of past-life regressions, and the in-between life regressions, and most stated they did not want to return to another incarnation. Even I had a couple of out-of-body experiences, and although they were not the same, I can understand why most did not want to return. Why would they? It is a paradise beyond description.

The Hebrew mystics returned to Palestine to continue these practices and called themselves the

Essenes. Many of the Gnostics were members of this group or were taught by them. The Essenes were said to have lived in privacy, in hermetically sealed compounds. They said they were living with, and being taught by, angels and extraterrestrials. They spoke of portals being opened in the sky, of flying craft, floating cities, and being taken into the heavens. This is what we today call abductions. Some investigators have said this was the first "true disclosure" that we are not alone in the universe. I stopped believing in coincidences decades ago. I find a great amount of synchronicity in the fact the Dead Sea Scrolls were discovered in 1947, and at same time we had the UFO crashes at Roswell. The Roswell crashes are important because this marked the time when humans began considering the idea we may not be alone in the cosmos. The Essenes also warned against an evil race of beings, from the cosmos. They called them the Arkon. They said they were trying to take over human consciousness, especially leaders, whether kings, politicians, or leaders of any large group of humans. They accomplished this by sending low-vibration forces of fear into their psyche. The fear would then increase the ego, which causes greed, the lust for power, and diminishes love, compassion, and empathy for others. The Apostle Paul wrote letters warning people of these beings and the forces of dark energy they send. They strongly suggested we stay away from these leaders and outside their influence. Clearly, this has continued to this day. In the second part of this book, I talked about the Draco Reptilians feeding on human fear, and how they have been controlling humanity, preventing us from awakening and from evolving in consciousness for centuries. I am convinced we are talking about the same race of beings. The Bible is full of references of reptiles, and so is ancient literature and artwork.

The Essenes and the Gnostics knew of the coming of the Messiah, of Jesus. They prepared for this for years. It is believed by researchers the Virgin Mary was an Essene and was prepared for the Holy Spirit to arrive and conduct the conception and incarnation of the baby Jesus. The New Testament gives us firsthand accounts of the teachings of Jesus and of the many "miracles" he performed. He told his disciples, "These miracles I perform, you, too, shall perform, and more." He taught us that love and forgiveness were the most important aspects of life. However, these teachings from his short ministry, in his flesh and blood body. We know that he returned, following his Resurrection. He continued to teach his disciples and the Gnostics. The Gnostic texts were about these teachings, from the "living Christ," in his celestial body. They seemed to be mostly about human ascension into the spirit world, how to again become light bodies, and how to navigate in the celestial world. This is where we learned that we have the divine spark, that we are each a fractal of light, of our Creator. We have forgotten who we truly are, and Jesus came here to help us remember. Gnostic is from the Greek word meaning "knowledge." Perhaps instead of us forgetting, we have been suppressed by the Arkon race spoken of in biblical times, or the Draco Reptilian we have learned about in the past few decades. I have discovered that all this information is connected, both in our pursuit of spiritual growth, the evolution of human consciousness, and the ET phenomenon. The fact is, millions of people worldwide are awakening to the truth. They are embracing the teachings of the Gnostics. These teachings have risen and fallen, several times over the past two thousand years. Even when the Dead Sea Scrolls were discovered in 1947, they were mostly suppressed for thirty to forty years. Since 1990, the word has proliferated globally. I have not yet learned the content of these writings in their entirety but am catching up fast. I can tell you there is a ring of truth in everything I have read. Besides, it is hard to argue the words written directly from the people who were there, followed Jesus, heard his teachings directly, both before and after his Resurrection.

They Gnostics said the Arkon filled us with the counterfeit spirit, that it hardened the human heart. This has resulted in many people thinking only with their head and with emotion. We should be thinking with our heart, which connect us to Christ consciousness, to universal consciousness. We then have access to all knowledge that has ever existed, as well as infinite wisdom. Because of this counterfeit spirit, or the demi-urge, we revere intellect. We place highly educated scholars and scientists on a pedestal. I am not suggesting this is wrong, but we should ask a question: Are these people connected to this universal consciousness too? We all know people who are so intelligent and highly educated, but without any common sense. We should be teaching everyone, especially our children, how to access their soul consciousness. By remaining in our head and belly, meaning our intellect and emotions, we have been held in this 3D reality of fear.

All the early mystics and philosophers, including the Essenes, Gnostics, Buddhists, Hindus, and Greeks, believed we can regain our "light bodies." They believed we could go back into the Garden of Eden and live in paradise. They believed would could escape the need to be reincarnated over and over. Personally, I think we return to continue to learn the art of love. Frankly, I do not believe anyone has the answers, and neither are we supposed to know. What I do know is that everything is connected, from the alien nonterrestrials, that visited and taught the people of India, to the Anunnaki from Sumerian, to the Essenes, etcetera. These were highly evolved civilizations, both spiritually and technologically. These teachings were not so much lost, but suppressed for centuries. We are just now rediscovering them. People worldwide are embracing them. In doing so, millions are now awakening and evolving in consciousness.

# 13

---

## VIRTUAL REALITY

---

Many centuries ago, science and religion parted company. Science concluded that we are all just matter, like machines. They believed that consciousness was just an artifact of brain activity. We are born, we live a few years, and then we die. Ashes to ashes and dust to dust. In contrast, religion told us of a life after life. Depending on how we have lived, we either go to heaven or to hell. The hard truth is that the separation of science and religion has left both impoverished. Neither were able to provide the answers to the questions people were asking. We need "both" to find the answers to our questions. Then around a hundred years ago, Dr. Albert Einstein had developed his theory of relativity, after which, quantum physics was born. Once again, science and religion seemed to be joined at the hip. Tom Campbell, a theoretical physicist, talked of his feelings toward religion, when he was just beginning his research, into consciousness, in his late twenties. He described himself as arrogant, a know-it-all, who saw religion as something for people full of fear, searching for answers to questions for which could never be answered. However, he said he soon learned that religions were all based in fundamental truth. Yes, most have been codified, filled with dogma. My God is better than your God. However, when you dig deep into the core of each, there is truth, the same truths. When I heard him say this, his credibility with me was instantly elevated. I have heard so many scientists and academics judge anyone who attends a church or believes in God.

I began hearing we were living in a virtual reality back in the 1990s. My shamanic teacher, Dr. Villoldo, suggested I watch the movie *The Matrix*. He said the movie would help me understand the reality we are living in. I have to say, thinking of the movie from that perspective scared me a little. I now know I was not alone in my fear, that many think it means the lives we live are not real, that this is a fake reality. As a result, as a way of facing my fear, I began my own investigation into this subject. I simply could not escape hearing we are in a virtual reality. Scientists have now proven this is true. However, as I began my quest, I soon learned this is not a modern-day concept. It has been around since ancient times. The Buddha said our reality is an illusion. They were saying the same things thousands of years ago, but with different terminology. I will now try and explain.

Today, we have virtual reality games, where the player wears a headset over their eyes. This produces the illusion they are in the game, as the avatar, which represents the player. I have never played one of them, but I understand it feels very real. Now this is not exactly the same thing as the virtual reality we all live in, but it provides a great framework for us to understand. Inside the game, everything feels real, but the key to understanding is to first realize the player is "outside the game itself." Now back to our daily virtual reality, which is the universe; everything we see, or experience, is based on how we interpret all the information, with our five senses. However, as in the game, the player must be outside, as consciousness. We are all consciousness, but we got fooled into believing we are our bodies, like the avatars in the game. While we live exclusively within the virtual reality, we only have access to information we gather from our five senses. When we awaken to who we truly are, consciousness, we suddenly have access to a wealth of information. We can get answers, guidance, and assistance in life from all consciousness. Knowledge and information give us true power. The virtual reality we see and experience is the physical universe. It is critical we awaken and remember who we truly are, that we are not physical; we are light, spirit, souls, fractals of light from God, whatever your conception may be. Again, the virtual reality is the physical world. The "real world," is consciousness; that is fundamental. It is the key to understanding all things. As I began to grasp this concept, I suddenly realized I did not feel so small anymore, so limited. We are so much more than anything we could have ever before imagined. This is because we are all netted together, all consciousness. Furthermore, the net of consciousness ties directly to our creator, which I call God. Tom Campbell is a physicist who has studied and researched consciousness for over forty years. His conclusions have been validated through the research of many others, like Gregg Braden. A few years ago, Tom did a short video. He pointed out the fact that most of us are constantly upset by what we see in the physical world: wars, people using people, the dishonesty, hatred, and a world full of fear. Most of us feel so powerless to do anything about it. He points out that these are all symptoms of a low quality of consciousness. He then explains the way to change the world is to "change ourselves." I not only completely agree with him, but I also know this is true, based upon my own life experience. No one can do this for you, or me. Governments and politicians certainly cannot help. They represent the symptoms of the problems. Besides, you cannot pass a law to dictate what is in a person's heart and soul. We must grow up and awaken to who we are. The first inner action is to begin removing our fears. Every negative symptom in the world has its roots in fear. Psychologists have said the biggest fear of all is the fear of death. Once we truly awaken to the fact that we are eternal, that we, consciousness, never die, the fear of death is diminished. We live our lives in fear. It is so pervasive, we do not even think about it. Much of it starts in childhood. Many parents have told their kids things like, "You are worthless," "You will never amount to anything," or "You cannot do this or that because you are not good enough." The list goes on and on. Another major fear is being rejected or fear "they" will not like me. The real problem is that so many of us do not love ourselves. We look for approval from others rather than approval from within our own souls. This is precisely why I have spoken so many times about the necessity of going within and the practice of rigorous self-honesty. By doing this, we begin to sort out the fears. *When we take away fear, we become love.* This is not easy and takes a long time, many lifetimes.

# 14

## THE AKASHIC RECORDS

When our physical bodies die, we enter the spirit world. One of the first things that happens is that we are taken to the Akashic records, which is like a database, your book of life. It consists of everything you have done in your most current life and all your past lives. This is where we have a "life review." I am told that we open our own book, but with the help of the people who are right for us. It might be parents, friends, Jesus, or even God. It is nonjudgmental, but we are shown everything we have ever done. However, it is mostly a review of our relationships to others. If you did good deeds, helped others, were loving, compassionate to others, you are shown how this felt from the other person's perspective. The flip side of this is that every time you hurt another person, lied to them, stole from someone, murdered, or physically harmed anyone, you then must relive it all from how it affected that person. If this is true, I would not want to be "in the shoes" of many people. Today, this is widely regarded as fact. There are countless professional and well-educated people researching this. For example, a man named Bill Foss has hypnotically regressed many people, helping them access their own records. He has a book out explaining how to access your own records. Scientist, doctors, and other professionals have proven the existence of these Akashic records, from experiencers of NDEs and psychiatrists performing hypnotic regressions. After the life review, you consider what you learned and what you still need to learn. This is done with the help of others, such as your angels or spirit guides. Then you choose your next incarnation, considering what you need to experience and learn. The bottom line is that we are all trying to learn the art of love, and to accomplish this, we must escape the bondage of fear.

As we evolve, lose our fears, and begin to love ourselves, and our neighbors, as ourselves, our vibration increases. We have long been stuck in this 3D, physical world. As we increase our vibration, we evolve out of the third density and into the fourth harmonic frequency. The fourth and the fifth are love-based frequencies. This is when we move into a new reality. We cease to see and experience all the pain, suffering, and chaos we see today. The "symptoms" disappear. This is why everyone is talking about our need to awaken and evolve in consciousness. We do have a choice. We can change the world. There will always be those who will reject change, but we do not need anywhere near 100 percent of the population to make this sift. We just need a critical mass. Once the shift happens, the others will follow.

We have all heard the expression "You cannot take it with you." We all know this is true, but think of all the billionaires that still want more and more. I have heard stories of these drug lords with rooms full of cash. I then wonder why they do not just quit, buy an island, and live happily ever after. Yet they never do, until they are either caught or killed. All these symptoms are examples of a low quality of consciousness, based in fear. Then I look at myself. I have been guilty of much of the same behavior. Like many of us, I have envied some of these people in the past. This is precisely why we must awaken to who we truly are. Once we begin to realize our reality is just an illusion, a simulated reality, and that we are so much more than we thought, we can only then begin to change and grow up. Everything I have written about here is just information. Today, humanity has access to more information than ever before in our history. The good news is that millions of people have awakened, or are in the process of awakening. This information is helping us to awaken to who we really are. It is indeed the answer, and the solution, to all the world's problems. As we evolve to a higher frequency, to the fourth harmonic level, we move away from fear and toward love. I grew up in a time where big boys did not cry. I was told I must "man up." This caused me to suppress my fears. Another point Tom Campbell made was that there is no such thing as the subconsciousness. Of course this differs from the Freudian model. He believes what we call the subconscious is all the fear we have suppressed. As we suppress our fears, or fear-based memories, we may begin the behave in destructive ways. We may then spend years in psychoanalysis, trying to uncover the fears. Here again, take away the fear and we are love. Imagine a man with an IQ of 180, but he is not evolved consciously. We would say he is a genius at that level. However, we have another man with an IQ of 125, but he has evolved consciously, and it is evident that he is much smarter, and wiser, than the genius. What this really means is that when we awaken to the fact that we are consciousness, get outside our heads, we then have access to universal, or Christ, consciousness. There is no limit to the amount of knowledge we have access to. We cannot measure this on an IQ scale. Earlier I spoke of a time when I began to think I was not so much learning new things but remembering. I now understand why I had felt this way. When I meditated, slowed my brain wave activity down, and got the brain out of the equation, I then had access to universal knowledge. We can all access this information. However, I confess, my struggle with this is, and has been, in getting my brain out of the loop. I find it difficult to switch my brain off. I find the only way I can accomplish this is to take myself into a deep meditation state.

# 15

## THE SHIFT IN
## CONSCIOUSNESS HAS BEGUN

The good news is that millions of people are making this shift in consciousness now. I know that some of you will want to just blow this off. It seems so deep and initially scared me. Then I realized there the fear was again controlling my life. I then heard a woman describing what it really means. First, she said that becoming fully awake, or aware, of who we truly are brings us into a state of perpetual love. The interesting thing is we do not have to go anywhere, reach a certain point in spiritual development, but just awaken and remember who we already are. This was a mind teaser for me, but I finally got it. In addition, we do not need to change anything in our outward lives, such as our careers, our marriage, or family. It is not some mystical thing only available to a few. This is already who we are in truth. We must cease to identify ourselves as the characters we have been playing in this game of virtual reality. By remembering that we are pure consciousness, light, and energy, we discover anything is possible. The virtual reality allows us to experience ourselves, to grow and evolve. Once we begin to realize we are all of the same light, from our Creator, we then become aware that harming someone else is harming ourselves. The 3D reality we perceive is real in that it gives us the opportunity to exercise free will, make choices, and learn from our mistakes. This is how we evolve to higher levels of conscious. This awakening will lead to an end of war, greed, violence, hatred, etcetera.

As I became more and more awakened to these truths, I wondered why it had taken me so long to hear this and to arrive at this realization. Like most everyone else, I had spent my life focused on earning a living, seeking happiness in the wrong things. I had practiced spiritual truths and followed the teachings of the Bible, my parents, and professors. I had completely missed, or perhaps just misunderstood, the deeper truth. I had learned we are all just energy, vibrating at a given frequency. I had seen quantum entanglement during my out-of-body experience in the jungle. I had several pieces of the truth but had never been able to connect the dots until now. I must tell you, I was somewhat shocked to learn that the enlightenment I had sought all those years and traveled around the world to find was already who I am. It was right under my nose the entire time. I now realize I had been looking outside myself for answers. The truth I sought was within me and within every one of us.

I know there will be a few people who read this book, that will think I am out in space, that I have lost my marbles. This always happens when we hear a new idea that differs with the narrative we have been taught and have lived. If you find yourself thinking like this, ask yourself these questions: Are you satisfied with how things are in the world today? Do you think we need to change, or that we cannot continue in the direction we are going? Why do we become angry when a new idea, or anything differing from our current paradigm of life, is introduced? It is all from fear. For example, in 1926, Nichola Tesla gave an interview. He said that one day the world would be a big brain, that we would be able to talk and see one another, anytime and anywhere in the world. He said everyone would have a device small enough to put in your breast pocket. He was laughed at, ridiculed, and accused of pseudoscience. Now almost a hundred years later, we refer to those devices as our cell phones. History has taught us that today's science fiction is tomorrow's science fact. Most everything in this book did not originate from me. I know that I am Harrison Nobody. Who am I to think I have the answers? Well, I tell you that you have access to the same information as I do. A few years ago,

I almost completely stopped watching Hollywood movies and began watching documentaries. I have recently noticed that, regardless of the topics, almost every single one of these experts in their respective fields are talking about awakening. These people include some of the most intelligent people on planet. Some are spiritual leaders, as you would expect. However, many are scientists, physicists, historians, anthropologists, ufologists, engineers, etcetera. Virtually all are saying we must awaken; we must evolve in consciousness. I have listened and learned pieces of truth from every one of them. Depending on the background of each, they may approach the truth from different perspectives, but they all arrive at the same conclusions. In the past, we have sought help with problems by turning to politicians, the economy, the military, and many similar sources. Where has this gotten us? In my opinion, not only are these directions for solutions not the answer, but also a huge part of the problem. The problem is not a political one; it is not an economic one. It is a spiritual problem resulting from a low quality of consciousness. To solve the problems, every one of us must awaken to our true selves and raise our conscious. There are methods to accomplish this, but we can begin with knowledge and correct information.

# 16

## AS ABOVE, SO BELOW

I had heard the expression "As above, so below" for years. I thought it meant as in heaven, it will be on earth. I was to discover I was on the right track to understanding, but it was far more complex that I had thought. In the end, it led me to a greater understanding of life, our relationship to each other and to everything in the universe. There is nothing we can find in the macrocosm that cannot also be found in the microcosm. Here are a few examples. First, look at the retina and iris of your eye. Then look at a picture of a nebula in the cosmos. They are virtually identical. Then there is my favorite; look at a microscopic picture of a human brain cell and then compare to a zoomed-out version of the universe. They appear identical. To give you one more, look at a picture of the birth of a cell, cell division, and then look at a supernova. The list goes on, and on. There is no way these comparisons are coincidences. Even when we view the inside of an atom, we have a nucleus, representing a sun, and the electrons, neutrons, and protons, encircling. This is just like a solar system. Everything is not only connected but everything in the universe is also constructed from the same blueprint.

These examples have led many to believe we are living in a fractal, holographic universe. This ties into the idea we are living in a simulated, or virtual, reality. There are many theoretical physicists who are convinced of this. I am told that Elon Musk believes this is a fact. The prefix "holo-" means whole. Each person, each part of the universe, is a part of the whole. I confess that my understanding of this is limited, but I find it amazing. We have all seen holographs, like the dove in the corner of a Visa card. However, in a large holographic image, if you break off one tiny corner, the little piece contains the entire image of the whole. Physicists say our 3D reality is a projection of light from the whole, located outside our known universe. Perhaps from God. We now know the universe is of light, of consciousness, and everything is connected. An analogy that helped me understand the idea of light projection is as follows: when we see a movie in a theater, we know that what we see on the screen comes from a roll of film, taken on a movie set, of real actors playing their role. It is captured on a film, which is in 2D. Then light is passed through the film, and it is projected onto a 2D screen. What we see are then 3D images, appearing on the large screen. This is not holographic, but it helps us to understand light projection effects.

Whether this makes complete sense to you, or to me, it does help to understand the nature of our 3D physical reality. Everything we see is on a scale. Now that we have had the Hubble telescope, and more recently, the launch of the James Webb telescope, we are able to see things in the universe that we could not have previously imagined. This has helped us to more fully comprehend the concept of "As above, so is below."

Many years ago, probably in the early 1990s, I heard a spiritual teacher say that we were gods. Initially, I took offense to that. I had been known for saying I only knew two things; first, there is a God, and second, I am not him. I later came to understand what he meant. We know the Bible tells us we were made in the image and likeness of God. This has nothing to do with skin color, eye color, gender, etcetera. God is our Creator, the Creator of the universe and everything within it. We are spiritual beings, individuations of God the Creator. We are each little creators, which is what the teacher was trying to say years ago. Each of us is responsible for creating the world around him or her. However, if we all get together, and work on creating something as a collective, then we have power. We now know that humanity is a highly creative species. I was listening to researcher Billy Carson explain a piece of this. He used the example of a cell phone. Before the first cell phone came into being, someone had a thought. Every new creation begins with a thought. Next he takes his thought to a draftsman, who puts a design on paper. Now the cell is in the second dimension. Then he takes it to an engineer, who builds a prototype that he can touch and hold. It is now in the 3D. It all began with the thought and then placed on a consciousness platform. Yes, we are all creators.

As consciousness, we are all connected to universal consciousness. We can pull ideas out of the ether, especially as we evolve in consciousness. I recently heard about a scientist who had discovered a "code" in the ether of space. It turns out this is the same code used in our search engines for our internet. Here is another example of how everything, and everyone is connected. The "strings" run through everything, and everyone in the universe.

I need you to know that I do not walk around thinking about string theory and the quantum field every day. Nor am I expecting anyone do this. I will leave this to the quantum physicists and researchers. What I am suggesting is simple. We must first realize we are indeed spiritual beings. We are consciousness having a physical set of experiences for the purpose of evolving, to learn the art of love. Every choice we make in our lives either helps us to evolve, or devolve. God and the universe want us to succeed. This takes time and a lot of experience. The biggest opponent to our success is *fear*. Decades ago, when I began my path in recovery, I now realize that much of what I was doing was facing my fears. This is why I placed so much emphasis on self-honesty. I had some fears I was conscious of and many that were buried deep within me. I previously had no idea of how fearful I had been. I was afraid to be myself, that others might not like me. I was afraid of failure and of success. I was always afraid that I was not worthy, not good enough. Today, I know of people, even some close to me, who are so full of fear and cannot see it in themselves. For example, if I begin telling them of things I have now realized, things in this book, they become angry. Anger is fear turned outward. The reason for their anger is because my suggestions could compel a deviation from the narrative of their own reality. Many call these people ignorant and narrow minded. I see them as lacking an open mind and being full of fear. This does not mean they are bad people, or even stupid people. Many just found an idea, or a belief, at some point in their lives and grabbed hold so hard they cannot consider they could have been misinformed, or more often, that they do not have the big picture. There is an old saying that "you are where you are." There should never be any judgment on those individuals whom have not yet evolved. Perhaps I should say they remain on the lower scale of the 3D reality. In every dimension, there are twelve octaves. I now know I have evolved into the fourth harmonic frequency, but when placed under stress I can revert downward, into maybe a 3-10. The people I have just been referring to are still in a solid 3D, maybe a 3-6 or a 3-8. I know of others who have evolved into the fifth harmonic frequency. As of today, humanity is evolving into the fourth harmonic. This is when we all become more spiritual, less self-centered, more compassionate, empathetic, and far less fearful. This is the "shift" everyone is talking about, insofar as consciousness. We must discover who we truly are, that we are all the same at our core being. Each of us is here to have our own set of experiences for the purpose of learning the art of love, love thy neighbor as thyself.

# 17

## BIBLICAL STORIES OF EXTRATERRESTRIALS

In the early 1970s, I read a book by Eric von Däniken called *Chariots of the Gods?* In retrospect, I think this marked the beginning of my quest for truth regarding the UAP phenomenon. I certainly came to believe we have been visited for thousands of years. He has since written several books and today is a widely known and respected researcher. He is a Christian man and studied the Bible for years. He had written a story about Ezekiel's wheel from the Old Testament, suggesting it was about an alien craft. Ezekiel was a high priest and described this vehicle coming down from the sky. Initially, he thought it was God and fell to his knees. He soon realized it was not God and described it as having metal legs and wheels that could turn in any direction, without any steering. To paraphrase the story, he was taken aboard and to a place high in a mountain. He looked below and saw a city with a temple. The craft lowered into this temple and fit perfectly. There he met a being who told him, "Humans have eyes to see, but you see nothing." He was then given a measuring device and asked to measure every part of the temple. Ezekiel did not know who they were but knew it was not God. In the original Hebrew version of this story, before translators got hold of it, the word God does not appear anywhere.

Sometime after Eric had written about this, he was invited to NASA to deliver a speech. This was kept secret. During the speech, he devoted about five minutes to the story of Ezekiel's wheel. Following his talk, they had a diner, and one of the engineering chiefs named Joseph Blumrich approached him. He told Eric there is no technology in the Bible. It was just a report of dreams and imagination. However, he decided to revisit the story and was amazed at the detail. So he literally designed and built a prototype of this flying device, which today we would call a space shuttle. It worked! A couple years later, a German engineer named Hans Herbert Blier had read von Däniken's book. He used the exact measurements and built a scale model of the temple. A short time afterward, Eric got Blumrich and Blier together. Each brought their scale model prototypes to a meeting. They were amazed to discover the flying shuttle fit perfectly in the compartment of the temple, just as Ezekiel had described it in the Bible. I must admit, this shocked me. Like most Christians, anything drawing a question to the validity of the Bible is generally offensive to me. However, there it was, in black and white, staring me in the eyes. I began thinking about it, using reason and logic. If UAPs and aliens are visiting us today, why should I be surprised they were around during biblical times? It had just never occurred to me. I had to adjust my thinking and open my mind. However, this story is not the only one, referring to extraterrestrials in the Bible.

Enoch, whose book was omitted from the Bible, talked of flying craft and of alien beings. He is mentioned this several times. This is likely why they did not include his book in the Bible, because of these references. The real problem in deciphering these stories is language. For example, there were several references to the heavens opening in the sky. Today, we call these portals, or a rip in the fabric of space. There are over three hundred verses in the Bible that refer to various descriptions of aliens or their vehicles. Among them are the following: stories of clouds as vehicles, pillars in the skies, dwellings as vehicles, lights on vehicles, spinning wheels, dark and shining vehicles, and flying furnaces. I have heard many researchers refer to the serpent in the Garden of Eden. They are convinced this is a reference to a Reptilian being. I spoke earlier in this book about the Arkon, whom the Apostle Paul warned us about. I believe he was talking about the

Draco Reptilians. They instilled fear in humans. The energy produced by fear is what they feed on. There are also references to flying serpents, and we now know that some species of the Reptilians have wings.

I must admit that some of this knowledge has bothered me. This is because it has produced deviation from the Christian narrative that I have lived my life by. However, nothing I have learned has produced a single question within me regarding my core belief in God and Jesus Christ. Going back to the Nag Hamadi texts, Dead Sea Scrolls, to the points made inside this chapter, not one piece of information has caused me to question my faith. Instead, it has broadened the scope of my understanding. To me, all that matters is the truth. The truth is the only path that will lead us to spiritual freedom and ascension. In the 1800s, British author and poet Lewis Carroll stated the following: "If you do not know where you are going, then any road will get you there." I choose the road of truth. Sometimes, the truth can be painful initially, but is always followed by peace and increased freedom of spirit. Yes, the truth will set you free.

# 18

## TRANSITIONING
## FROM WITHIN

In part B of this book, I will provide a wealth of evidence to you that we are not alone in the universe. Statistics now tell us that at least 80 percent of the population now believe that other life exist in the cosmos. Although I know some readers may reject this, the day is coming when you will be confronted with this fact. We are missing so much of our human history, one that shows that extraterrestrials have not only visited this planet but have lived here. Furthermore, there is proof they lived and worked with us, teaching us the rudiments of civilization. Scientist tell us the earth is 4.5 billion years old. Our mainstream history books suggest that civilization began only five to six thousand years ago. Clearly, looking at the big picture, we see that is like the blink of an eye. Still, the reality we have known exists only withing that short period of time.

God gave all of us free will, so everyone is free to believe what they choose. Still, the fact remains that the ET phenomenon is accepted as a fact. Even the government no longer denies it. Every insider I have ever heard agrees a disclosure event is imminent. It will "shift" human consciousness and change our known reality virtually overnight. Regardless of what you choose to believe, "the shift" I am referring to is happening now. We will awaken to the fact that we are consciousness and we are connected to all consciousness in Gods universe. We are not different but the same. Only the truth can free us from the suffering and the chaos of the world we live in. Only truth can free us from those who are controlling us, and who have been for centuries. This has occurred so gradually that most of us have not noticed. We just accept our reality as normal. Only "we the people" can awaken and choose a new and wonderful reality. We have been lied to for so long, at least since WWII.

Please believe me: I am not trying to tell anyone what to believe. I only provide a mountain of truth. It is left to you whether to accept or reject. I ask only one thing: please keep an open mind.

# PART B

# 19

## UNDENIABLE EVIDENCE

Over the years, I have heard many people who question the existence of extraterrestrial life ask, "Where is the proof?" In fact, there is so much proof, I have been overwhelmed. Perhaps some are willing to discount the hundreds of thousands of eyewitnesses worldwide. Although this is a stretch, but then how do you discount the endless string of verified government documents on this subject?

We have heard of many crashed UFO incidents, going back to the 1940s. They have been denied by our government. We now know this was all orchestrated with a methodical technique. In the early 1980s, a top-secret document was leaked. It was a special operations manual, called SOM-101. The title was *Extraterrestrial Entities Technology Recovery and Disposal.*

The document described several ET races and

instructions on the process to recover crashed space-craft. Perhaps most important, it provided specific guidelines on how to maintain secrecy, from the public and journalists. To put it concisely, it gave orders on ways to deal with eyewitnesses by ridiculing them and destroying their credibility. The late Dr. Stanton Friedman got his hands on a copy and contacted Dr. Robert Wood, asking him to validate the authenticity. He did validate, even locating the printing press from where it originated, at Kirtland AFB. Since that time, many experts have reviewed the documents, and all have concluded it is real. In addition, we know that since the early 1950s, this is precisely the methodology used. If anyone had a valid UFO sighting, they were ridiculed and turned into a joke. The witnesses either ceased talking about it, or their lives were destroyed. Some disappeared, never to be seen again. The government has never denied the validity of the SOM-101 training manual.

In 1983, award-winning science journalist Linda Moulton Howe was doing research on the UAP phenomenon. She was invited to Kirtland Air Force Base, where she met with then AF intelligence agent Richard Doty. She was taken into an empty room, with a single chair, and handed a document. She was allowed to read and ask questions, but was not permitted to write anything down. Inside the document she read that thousands of years ago, EBENs (extraterrestrial biological entities) manipulated DNA in already evolving primates to create homo sapiens. In the last part of the document, it talked about Project Garnet. The final statement was as follows: all questions and mysteries about the evolution of homo sapiens on this planet have been answered. This project is closed. It was obvious this had shaken Linda up. She later verified this information when interviewing the air force officer, who was the handler of a captured EBEN from the Roswell crash. This really shook me up too. However, I have since learned the EBENs were only one race of beings that tinkered with our DNA. Evidence today proves there were at least twelve races engaged in this.

In 2017, the *New York Times* did a front-page story, and the US Navy released videos of what is now called UAPs, unidentified aerial phenomenon. For the first time in history, the topic is being discussed in mainstream media. Whistleblowers are coming out of the woodwork. The government has not acknowledged the existence of other life in the cosmos, but neither are they denying it. They do not appear to care who talks about UAPs, or alien life. Today, a government insider can speak out and reveal what they know on this subject. Twenty years ago, the ones that did this had to risk everything, their credibility, their careers, and their lives. Still, many did just that. They received no money and knew beforehand they would be subjecting not only themselves, but also their family and friends, to horrible things. Why did they choose to go public? Virtually every one of them said they felt strongly the public had a right to know. They felt this story was far too big to keep secret. They had person-ally witnessed the depth of the lies and conspiracy within this cover-up. Many have seen technology that could forever change our lives—medical technology that can cure all disease and free energy devices that would give us back clean air and water. They were will-ing to risk their lives to shine light on the truth. In my mind, these people are real heroes.

# 20

## WE ARE NOT ALONE

Earlier in this book, I spoke of an approaching new reality. I spoke of how excited I was. To reach this forthcoming reality, the most important shift is human awakening. We must raise our consciousness before any of these beautiful things can occur. Depending on your current knowledge level, when you finish reading the information contained in the following chapters, your consciousness will be expanded. You will never think of the universe in the same way.

The second shift to come is the "disclosure event." By this, I mean disclosure of the truth, that we are not alone in the cosmos. In fact, the universe is teeming with life. The amount of evidence is overwhelming. For a few people, this is still a very controversial topic. However, my goal is to bring truth. Statistics show that today most Americans believe in extraterrestrial life. Yet I have friends, whom I have great trust and respect for, who reject this idea outright. I want all readers to know that I am not here to judge anyone's beliefs, nor to disrupt the paradigm they live by. Instead, I refer to the age-old statement that "the truth will set you free." The fact is, the truth on the subject is going to be revealed. It is already happening. To deny this is to disagree with virtually every scientist, military leader, astronaut, and US president since FDR. I have done thousands of hours of research on this topic in the past few years. I must tell you that I have never seen an alien craft, nor had a close encounter. I sure would like to. I have never seen God, nor Jesus, but I know he walked among us on the earth. For me, I have listened to so many eyewitnesses and taken the time to dig deep into the mountains of evidence, I now accept extraterrestrial life as reality.

As I reflect on my life, I think I have always known of other life in the cosmos. I agree with the scientists who say it is stored in our DNA. Humans have been looking at the stars since ancient times. Then the first telescopes came into being, which allowed astronomers to see other planets in our solar system. Galileo developed the first rudimentary telescopes in the 1500s. When the space age began, new telescopes were designed, such as the Hubble telescope, which was launched outside our atmosphere. The Hubble allowed us to see far into the universe. More recently, we have the new

James Webb telescope, which is far more powerful than the Hubble. We know that our solar system is part of the Milky Way galaxy. If we traveled in a straight line, linearly, it would take many lifetimes to cross. Now are you ready for this? With the new telescopes, astronomers now say there are two hundred trillion galaxies. That is right—two hundred trillion. In my mind, to believe that humans are the only sentient beings in the universe is insane. I cannot conceive that we could be alone. I not only believe in other sentient life in the universe but am also convinced they have been visiting earth for thousands of years. All one needs to do is visit ancient sites, like the Great Pyramids at Giza, Stone Henge in England, Machu Picchu in Peru, or Teotihuacan in Mexico. The list goes on to include countless other sites all over the world. I have visited a few of the sites, and it is inconceivable they could have been built by human hands alone. Certainly not with the tools and technology of the time. I have seen the architecture with my own eyes. Many people have seen photos of these sites, but believe me, it is difficult for a photograph to capture the intricate details of the construction. The impact it had on me was incredible. I saw walls built of stones that were as large as trucks, weighing many tons. They were connected to smaller stones at every angle and fitted together so tightly that lichen would not grow between them. Because you cannot carbon-date stone, we can only guess the age of these structures. Many modern engineers have tried to duplicate the construction of this architecture and failed miserably, even with current technology.

In the 1970s, a researcher named Hans Jenny proved that sound frequences alter matter, including stones. This is the study of cymatics. Today, many scientists believe that structures like the Great Pyramids of Giza, and the other stone sites I mentioned, were materialized by sound out of thin air. There is a documentary online, by Jenny, that provides proof of this concept. I must admit it makes sense because to date, no one has been able to figure out how these sites could have been constructed.

We have countless stories, written information, petroglyphs, and artwork, all depicting alien visitations. Egypt is full of history, as is India in their Veda texts. They speak of flying craft and alien beings, they called gods. We have learned a lot from the Sumerian text of ancient Mesopotamia. They spoke of beings they called the Anunnaki, which translated means those who came from the stars, or the heavens. Many thought the Anunnaki were just one race, but there were several. A man named Zechariah Sitchen spent his life translating the Sumerian text. According to him, the Anunnaki tinkered with human DNA. Today, there is "clinical proof" that someone did. I will get back to this later. Whatever the truth is, one fact is clear: we are missing thousands of years in human history. Many historians, geologists, and researchers have dedicated their lives to the understanding of ancient civilizations. I could write several books on the information I have learned, but triple that number on what I do not know. There are so many differing opinions and so much conjecture, which led me to conclude that no one knows for sure. What is important is they all agree on at least two major points. First, the earth has gone through several cycles, often ending with catastrophic events, such as the great flood. Each time, humanity had to start over, which is what I fear will happen if we fail to awaken and to evolve in consciousness. The second thing all these researchers agree on is that we have been visited by extraterrestrial races many times. They have indeed been helping us throughout time. God knows we need it.

# 21

## BEGINNING OF MODERN
## UAP REPORTS

In more modern times, we have had sightings of unidentified flying craft, going back hundreds of years, to the fifteenth and sixteenth centuries. The Bible is full of references to their existence. There was a crashed UFO in Aurora, Texas, in 1898, on a farm. There was an alien body discovered. The local people even held a Christian funeral service for the entity. This was reported in a Dallas newspaper at the time. No one freaked out, which is interesting when you consider that those in charge of disclosure today are so afraid that we cannot handle the truth. We are far better prepared today than we were in the nineteenth century. In February of 1942, we had a major event, called "the battle of LA." This was witnessed by around a million people. The shore batteries fired every shell they had, as did our warships in the harbor. The craft never fired back. They had eight huge spotlights on it, which appeared in the papers the following day. According to the late William Thompkins, who witnessed the event, there were multiple crafts, which most did not notice. At least one crashed in the ocean and was recovered by the US Navy. This was the beginning of back-engineering by the navy. This occurred only about three months after Pearl Harbor. This was also the beginning of government denial. They tried to explain it away as war nerves. Then they claimed it was a weather balloon. This was insane, and the army became infuriated because it suggested they could not discern the difference between a weather balloon and a flying craft. Even worse, that even with thousands of shells, they failed to bring it down. As the war progressed, our pilots began reporting that they were seeing what came to be known as "foo fighters." This was occurring in both the European and the Pacific theaters of war. Both the Allies and the Axis powers were seeing them. This came to the attention of General Douglas MacArthur. He then ordered then General Jimmy Doolittle to investigate and get back to him. After some time, General Doolittle reported back that we had "spectators" to the war. They never became involved, never fired at any of our planes; they just observed. He concluded they were not of earthly origin. After the war, in 1955, General MacArthur stated that our next wars would be with other planets. What I have a problem with regarding his statement is this: he knew these alien craft had not once exhibited any hostility. Yet he jumped to the conclusion we will have to go to war with them. Even to this very day, almost every time this topic arises, it is accompanied by the word "threat." This is fear of the unknown. In my humble opinion, this is one of the most concerning flaws in human character; we fear what we do not understand. Over the past eight decades of continuous sightings of alien craft, there is no evidence to suggest they are hostile. The only time they have interacted with our war machines has been for self-protection. Even then, our military has called "them" hostile. With all due respect to our military, many of them are like the proverbial hammer; everything they see is a nail. There have been many governmental studies conducted on this subject. Every one of them has concluded they do not present a threat to national security, but they did not once say they do not exist.

Before I move further into this subject, I want to put a couple of things into perspective. First, I realize there are people who reject the idea of extraterrestrial life. It disrupts the narrative they have lived their lives by. In fact, this was true for me and most of us. However, we cannot change what is! I have spoken and written that the key to inner peace and happiness is based in honesty. Anything built on lies, whether a marriage or a country, is doomed to fail. Alcoholism is called a disease of denial. Many times, everyone else knows except the alcoholic. There can be no relief until the alcoholic reaches a point of acceptance of the truth and becomes willing to change. The same holds true with those who deny the existence of alien life in the cosmos. I say this to the reader; whether you are ready to accept the existence of ET presence or not, I ask: How do you feel about being lied to? I have invested years, thousands of hours, investigating this subject. Initially, it was mostly curiosity on my part. However, as I learned more, I realized how these lies have harmed us. Just this morning, I was talking with a friend, and this subject came up. I quickly realized he was not very interested. In fact, he asked, "How does this affect my life?" I could not judge him because in the beginning, I had felt the same way. As you read further, you will begin to understand just how much it affects all our lives. This will become very relevant to you when you discover the technology, from reverse engineering, that exists in the medical arena. We are suffering from diseases, cancer, and so many physical problems today. The technology is there right now that would cure virtually every disease known to man. I had a "below the knee" amputation a few years ago. It resulted from an accident in the gym. I have a prosthesis and can do most things I want. Still, it is a challenge to live with every day. I have never regretted having it done nor complained. I refuse to be a victim. The only time I have felt anger is when I discovered the technology exists today to grow a new foot for me. Using my own DNA, they can either grow one or 3D print one for me. This technology has been around for over thirty years at least. Why is this and other medical technology being withheld from us? Ultimately, I can answer this in one word: greed! I can take this one step further. My friend asked me, "Does this not hurt the greedy people in control? They are human and get sick too." The answer is no, it does not affect them. This is because they have direct access to this technology. They have no compassion for the rest of us. Clearly, compassion is not part of their reality.

# 22

## WWII: DID WE REALLY WIN?

Earlier, I mentioned the "battle of LA," in early 1942. I also spoke of the presence of "foo" fighters in WWII, as they were called. There was something else taking place, before and during the war, something that affects us to this day. This has to do with what the Nazis were doing. Everyone knows we beat the Germans in the war. I was shocked to learn that we did not beat the SS component of the Nazis. Initially, not only was I shocked but had a difficult time believing it. I ask you to stay with me, as I try and explain. There are two angles on this. First, in 1922, there was a young woman named Maria Orsich in Germany. She was a psychic and wanted to leave Earth. This was just after WWI, and Germany was truly suffering. She psychically connected to an alien race in another star system. The story is that she received downloads of blueprints, into her mind, on how to build a starship. She went to a university, where she connected with a professor who helped her to build this flying craft. She had help from a small group of women who also possessed psychic abilities. The craft was built, and it worked. Later, in 1933, the Nazis came into power. It is well known that Hitler had people going all over the world searching for ancient technology. They learned about Maria and allowed her to continue her work, separate from the military. She did not want any craft built by her and her friends to be used for war, only travel. Himler was head of the SS and they were into the occult. They were members of the "Briel society." To make a long story short, they eventually connected to an alien race, known as the Reptilians, in Antarctica. They formed an alliance with these Draco Reptilians, who shared an unbelievable amount of technology with them. This included flying craft. They eventually moved everything to Antarctica, to these huge underground caverns. This occurred well before the end of the war. Many now say this was the first "breakaway" civilization. You may be asking where I heard of these stories? It began through a man I mentioned earlier, William Thompkins. He was a brilliant young man in the navy during this time. He reported directly to Admiral Ricca Botta, who in turn reported to the secretary of the navy, William Forrestal. Admiral Botta was handling the German-speaking covert operatives, working inside Germany, gathering intelligence. There were twenty-nine of these men, working as spies. When they began returning to report what they had learned, no one would believe them. Every one of them had been witness to this incredible technology, obviously not of earthly origin. At the time, no other country knew of the presence of alien life on Earth. Each of these operatives knew no one would believe them. Each worked separately, with no knowledge of what the others were seeing. Eventually, after hearing the same reports from every single one of these men, Admiral Botta and Admiral Forrestal were compelled to accept this as truth. Bill Thompkins was one of only a couple individuals who were present at the debriefings. He carried the reports to Forrestal. This was incredible news to me. Several years ago, I was addicted to the history of WWII. I watched thousands of hours of documentaries and read everything I could get my hands on. I had never heard any of this. I have now verified this information through several sources and must conclude it is all true.

# 23

## 1947: WHAT A YEAR IT WAS

Now let us move forward to 1947. This may be one of the most important years in recent history. First, in July of that year, there were two UFO crashes in New Mexico. The one everyone heard of is known worldwide as the Roswell crash. However, the government insiders refer to it as the Corona crash. This is because it occurred close to Corona, New Mexico. It was later removed to Walker Army Airfield in Roswell. There were two craft that had collided, during a bad electrical storm. The second craft was not found until 1949 by some ranchers near a place called Horse Mesa, in the middle of nowhere. To this day, no one knows exactly what caused these crashes. Earlier that year, a pilot named Kenneth Arnold spotted a group of flying disks in Washington State. His description led to the use of the term "flying saucers."

Although there had been other crashes prior to 1947, this appears to be when the secrecy, and the cover-up began in a formal manner. Harry Truman was president and was informed about what had happened. It was also that year the CIA was formed and the former army air force was split, and the US Air Force was formed. He had appointed William Forrestal as the very first secretary of defense. Truman then directed Forrestal to form a group to investigate and oversee the UFO phenomenon. This group became known as the Majestic Twelve, or MJ-12. They became the deep, dark insiders on the investigations. I will come back to the Corona crash soon but need to tell you of another major incident that also occurred in 1947.

William Forrestal knew about what the Nazis had been doing, as I described earlier. They knew that the Nazis had moved to Antarctica and set up bases under the ice. So Admiral Richard Byrd was ordered to lead a flotilla of our best ships down there to flush them out. You can look this up. It was called "Operation High Jump." The inside story is they were planning to be down there for six months but came back after five weeks. They had fought a battle and suffered great loses, approximately 30 percent of the ships and hundreds of sailors. According to William Thompkins and a few others, they encountered "flying saucers," that came up from under the ocean, from two directions. From one side there were Nazi craft that had the swastika markings. From the other direction came several other craft, including some that were "cigar" shaped, with no markings. Thompkins had seen several photos. Clearly, the unmarked craft were of the Reptilian Fleet. To be more specific, they were the "Draco Reptilians," which are the worst race, enemies of humanity and other races in the cosmos. They go with the Nazis from planet to planet, enslaving the inhabitants and stealing everything. The Draco seem to constitute most of the evil inhabitants of our galaxy, but not all.

At the first UFO crash, near Corona, New Mexico, they found five extraterrestrials. All were dead except one. He was taken to Los Alamos, where he lived until 1952. He was called EBE-One, with EBA meaning extraterrestrial biological entity. He was very cooperative and tried to explain the technology, but our scientists could not understand at that time. Communication with him, and he was a male, was initially almost impossible. He tried teaching them his language to no avail. He did write down his alphabet, which consisted of over thirty characters. Years later some linguists managed to grasp enough to do basic communication. Around 1949, a doctor at Los Alamos implanted a device in his throat that would allow him to speak English, which he quickly learned. His intelligence level was far beyond that of any human. We have two lobes in our brain, but he had twenty-two lobes. He tried to explain the propulsion system on his craft and many other technologies present. Our physicists could not understand his explanations because he was using physics that were unknown to them. He also told them about the communication system on board. He wanted to send a message home, to ask his people to come and get him. He died in 1952, but had taught them how to use the communication device. They were then able to send messages to his home planet, code named Serpo. It is 39.5 light-years from Earth, in the Zeta Reticuli star system.

# 24

## OPERATION SERPO

By 1964, our people had arranged an exchange program with the EBENs. This was called Operation Crystal Night, but most people know it as Operation Serpo. We selected twelve astronauts to go. There is some disagreement on how many went. The original documents stated there were twelve, but other sources say only three went. I tend to think it was twelve. They underwent a massive amount of training, but the question is, How do you train someone for a mission like that? Anyway, in 1965, the EBENS landed. They left one of their people here and took our people with them. From what I have been told, EBA-2, as he was called, is still here to this day. The trip from earth to Serpo took nine months. They lived on Serpo for twelve to thirteen years, returning in 1977. The debriefing report was very detailed. They were treated exceptionally well. The only problem they encountered was in the fact that Serpo is situated in a binary star system. The temperature was very hot, and it was almost never dark. This could explain why the EBENs never sleep, only rested. Because of the increased levels of radiation, they were getting sick. After a year, the EBENs moved them to the northern part of the planet. Following this move, they were much more comfortable. There is a lot more detail, but for my purposes here, it is enough for you to know this did happen. Once they returned, many had developed cancers and died after a few years. The commander lived longest. He died only a few years ago. He had spoken at a couple of UFO conventions and was said to have been a great speaker. He had nothing but the highest respect for the EBEN race. I am aware this is a fantastic story, but I am inclined to believe it. What I can tell you is that I got this information from multiple, highly respected sources. It is incomprehensible to me that all of them would have made this up. Although I did not go deep into the details here, I cannot imagine that this could have been fabricated. There were just too many specific details in the debriefing reports. The person whom I heard this story from said he saw several photographs of Serpo, the planet. He said the first photos were taken at their original landing site. He said it appeared desertlike. The northern region, where they were relocated to after a year, had trees, streams, and a few species of animal life. He said the

EBENs lived in adobe-style homes. Our people had freedom to go anywhere they wanted, with two exceptions. They were not allowed to enter any of the homes. Secondly, the EBENs held a worship service every day, which they were not allowed to attend. They did have a deity, but our people could not find out more than that. During the years they were there, one member of the team died in an accident, while trying to fly one of the EBEN craft. The EBENs took the body, and our people wanted it back for burial. Initially, they were denied. This caused some conflict. However, the EBENs had a negotiator, who spoke English and settled the issue. They got his body back. When they were taken to retrieve the body, they entered a large building. Inside it was filled with "vats," all containing bodies that were being cloned. Their man was inside one of the vats. The EBENS then helped them with the burial service. e tried teaching his languageHHe

The 1950s were active years, with many incidents regarding this phenomenon. First, in 1952, there were several UFOs that flew over Washington. This occurred over two consecutive weekends. Many refer to this as the "Washington UFO Flap." These craft were tracked on radar and seen by thousands of people. They scrambled our fastest fighter jets of the time, which I think were F-89s. They failed to even get near them. The speeds were beyond anything we could imagine. Anyone of the time, and to this day, would think there was no way our government could deny or cover this up, but they did. The following year, the Robertson Panel was put together to discuss the UFO phenomenon. They returned with a report that said these flying craft posed no threat to the national security of the United States. What was not disclosed were their proposed measures to handle this issue with the public. Basically, the plan was not to explain these sightings, but to explain them away. When an event occurred, one they could not explain, they would ridicule the people that exposed it, making them look like idiots. However, in cases where this did not resolve the situations, they went far beyond harassment and ridicule. There were a few cases where witnesses vanished, never seen again. It is clear these people would stop at nothing to protect this secret, and I do mean nothing. Had they just told us the truth in 1947, or after the flyover in Washington, we would not have the problems we are facing today. Had they been honest, the world we live in today would be beyond belief. I am confident that the SOM-101 training manual on how to handle these events was a result of the Robertson Panel. The dates match perfectly, connecting both the panel meeting and the printing of SOM-101.

# 25

## ALIEN VISITATION AT THE

## PENTAGON AND WHITE HOUSE

There are many people who reject the idea of ET life because of their religious beliefs. The insiders sitting in think tanks, discussing the disclosure topic, have many concerns on how the truth might impact religions. There are some good reasons. For example, we now know that some ET groups tinkered with our DNA many years ago. It is also well established that many of our ancestors interfaced with ETs, their technology, and misunderstood them for gods. There are many accounts of this in the Bible and in every major religion on earth. I must admit, when this knowledge first became known to me, I was upset. It took a few years for me to sort it out in my own mind. First, the amount of evidence that they tinkered with our DNA is overwhelming. However, this has to do with our physical body, which is not who we are. If you recall the earlier portion of this book, we are not our bodies. We are fractals of light, from our Creator. Now is a good time to inject another truth; we are indeed light beings, all connected. But this does not only pertain to life on Earth, but all sentient life in the universe. We are all connected, and our alien visitors have known this for millions of years. They were once where we are, in our evolution, and most of them are here in a benevolent way, trying to help us.

Around twenty-five years ago, I heard a story while watching a documentary. This story has heled me to accept many components of the extraterrestrial phenomenon. Many people ask, "If the aliens are real, then why do they not just land on the White House lawn?" Well, in 1957, they sort of did this. An alien craft landed in the Arlington, Virginia, area. The local police saw this and went to the craft. A man appeared from inside the craft, asking to be taken to the president, who was Eisenhower at that time. They first took him to the Pentagon and later to the White House. His name was Valient Thor, and he was from the planet Venice. He met with President Eisenhower, Richard Nixon, the cabinet, and other advisers to the president. He explained that he represented a Galactic Federation of planets. He explained they had great concern about our nuclear weapons. Commander Thor then explained he had a deal to offer us. Essentially the deal was this: if we agreed to dispose of all our nuclear weapons, they would give us free energy and offer us medical technology that would eliminate all diseases and human suffering. He said they were making the Soviet Union the same offer. These technologies would be made available to the entire planet. I do not know how long these discussions went on. I do know that Commander Thor lived in an apartment at the Pentagon for three years. In the end, inexplicably, his offer was rejected. Supposedly, Eisenhower was in favor of doing this and was planning to go to the United Nations with it. The rejection was from all the people around him. They were worried that free energy and medical care would destroy the economy. It certainly would have destroyed the gas and oil industry. Now would that not be just be too bad? We would have clean air and water. This story has never been denied. I have seen interviews of Eisenhower's granddaughter, and she says it is true.

During his time living at the Pentagon, he was searching for one good soul. He later stated that he had never been in a place where there was so much mental chaos, concentrated in one spot. He did find one secretary who assisted him in arranging a meeting with Dr. Frank E. Stranges, who was a minister. This was the beginning of a lifelong series of meetings between Thor and Stranges. Dr. Stranges later wrote some books. One is entitled *Stranger at the Pentagon*. I have read this book a couple of times and have a copy on my desk right now. Whatever you choose to believe,

I strongly encourage you to obtain and read this book. I say this because of what is coming, and what everyone on this planet will be faced with. I would go so far as saying that if you are a Christian, or even lean toward the Christian faith, reading this book is a must. Val told Frank that on his planet, and on many others, they have never broken God's laws. He said that Jesus Christ is the first, and the last, the alpha and the omega. It is important to understand that Valient Thor is a light being. He looks and appears just like one of us. In Dr. Stranges's book, there are several photos of him. He can dematerialize and rematerialize at will. I do not recall if he revealed the average lifespan of the people on Venice, but it must be over two thousand years. This is common in the universe. We humans have very short lives. For them, everything is about love. We must wake up and grow up. This is exactly what the countless numbers of alien species are waiting on us to do. They are truly concerned about us continuing in a war footing. During the Cold War, it was called "MAD," mutually assured destruction. Mad is a good name for it because it was absolute insanity. I ask you to think about this. A politician can press a button and everything, and everyone, ceases to exist. No one wins. This is a chess game that is still being played to this day.

# 26

## ET VISITS TO OUR NUCLEAR SITES

It was immediately after WWII when UFOs began showing up everywhere, especially around military bases, where nuclear weapons were stored. There were crashes and sightings in New Mexico. Why were there so many unidentified craft in that state? First, the atom bomb was made at Los Alamos, tested in White Sands, and the only bomb group in the world qualified to carry and drop the bomb was in Roswell. This was the 509th Bomb Group. They were the ones who investigated the "Roswell crash," and later the army asked us to believe these people, with high security clearances, could not discern the difference between a flying craft and a weather balloon. The reports of alien craft over these sites continue to this day. They have done everything from switching them off to rendering them useless. This has occurred, not only in this country, but also all over the world. It is important to note that during these events, they have never harmed a single person, nor shown any kind of aggression. Many have said it is obvious they are sending us a message. Frankly, I find it comforting. They know where every nuclear weapon in the world is located. The message has been crystal clear: if we attempt to use one of them, they will stop it. They have also informed us that igniting a nuclear weapon on this planet also has a negative impact on them and other dimensions. Commander Thor tried to explain this to our Pentagon officials. A former military officer named Robert Salas, who worked at Maelstrom AFB, deep inside the nuclear command center, has testified publicly about them shutting down all the missel silos back in the 1960s. This story has gone viral and is known worldwide.

# 27

## WHO KILLED JOHN KENNEDY?

In the years that followed, Dr. Stranges spoke all over the world, to groups of scientists, ufologists, and many others on the subject. His life was threatened numerous times. The dark forces came close to taking him out a couple of times, but Commander Thor or his people were always there to save him.

John Kennedy became president in 1961. He was well informed about alien life. He made a lot of enemies. A major decision he had made was to withdraw all our troops, called advisers, from Vietnam, by the end of 1963. This really upset the military industrial complex and the CIA. They had already made plans to fight a war. He also wanted to disclose the truth on alien life in the cosmos. Of course, we all know he was assassinated in Dallas on November 22, 1963. This was a terrible thing, not just for the obvious reasons, but we lost our innocence that day. Had he lived, we would have had a very different reality. The Vietnam War would have never been fought. Probably, disclosure would have taken place before he left office. I was a young boy, in junior high school, but his death left a huge impression on me that has continued to this day. I could write a book on what I have learned about the truth of that day. There have been countless numbers of documentaries and researchers, all claiming to have the answer as to who was behind this. Most everyone will tell you that Lee Oswald did not act alone. Many believe, and I am one of them, that he did not fire a gun that day. I have heard theories that it was any of a long list: the Mafia, the FBI, CIA, Secret Service, the Soviets, and Castro. It is clear to me that there were several involved, not only in killing Kennedy but also even more in the cover-up.

Lyndon Johnson was immediately sworn in as the next president. He appointed a commission to investigate, called the Warren Commission. After some time, they returned the results, which stated that Lee Harvey Oswald was solely responsible. Bobby Kennedy had already begun his own investigation. He knew about Valient Thor and that Frank Sturges was still in contact with him. Frank said that one day a long caravan of several cars showed up at his house, and Bobby Kennedy came in. Franks said his entire neighborhood was watching. He asked Dr. Sturges to ask Val Thor who was responsible for his brother's death. Frank agreed but explained he had no way of knowing when, or if, he would show up again. Bobby gave him a phone number to call if he got an answer. As it turned out, Thor did show up soon thereafter. Frank told him the story and asked him the question "Who was behind the JFK killing?" Frank was expecting a list of individuals, but without hesitation, Thor gave him one name. I have heard from many reliable sources that many of the ETs know everything about us, each one of us. They have technologies that allow them to observe everything we do. I had heard the story of Valient Thor and Frank Sturges many years ago. Last year, I was watching an episode of Cosmic Disclosure on Gaia TV. Emery Smith was interviewing a man named Michael Jaco. Michael had spent over twenty years on SEAL Team 6 and another eleven years in the security forces of the CIA. He has also been in the secret space force for most of his life. He shared a story pertaining to a portion of his early training, which connected me back to the Valient Thor story. Gaia vets every guest thoroughly. They had brought in Dr. Barbara Lamb, a world-renowned hypno-regression therapist. They showed video of her sessions with Michael. He stated that when he was approximately twenty years old, he was taken to the planet Venus, on one of their spacecrafts. We have all heard that the surface of Venus is extremely hot, that no human life could survive. Valient

Thor had said they lived under the surface. Michael said they landed, and it was eighty-five degrees on the surface. Perhaps they had terraformed this one area. He was then taken underground, where there were cities of such beauty, he could barely comprehend. He was one of fifteen Americans sent there. The purpose was for consciousness training. What he described was beyond incredible. Everyone and everything on the planet was of a love frequency. The people were beautiful, but taller than most humans. A short person there was six feet, and some were nine to ten feet tall. The first thing they taught him was to lose his fear. Then he was taught to shift his vibration to communicate with everything, via a love vibration. He learned to communicate with animals, plants, and everything. He said that every person, plant, animal, and even the water, had a love vibration. He said that many of our philosophers had been trained by them. He also said that many ET races came there for training. I cannot imagine. It sounds like heaven. Michael said leaving there was very difficult.

# 28

## EISENHOWER'S FINAL MESSAGE AND MURDER OF WILLIAM FORRESTAL

I admit these stories blew me away. However, it is much easier to understand when you consider human civilization is said to be only a few thousand years old. Then compare with many ET civilizations that are tens of thousands, and even millions of years beyond ours. It then becomes easier to contemplate. Just look how far our technology has evolved in the past one hundred years, even the past fifty years. What if you tried to explain a smartphone to someone from a hundred years ago? These ET civilizations are so far advanced, we must look like Stone Age people to them. However, this evolution is not only in technology but in spirituality, and especially in consciousness evolution. If you consider these facts, these stories are a little more believable. In fact, if they were not fantastic, they would not be believable. Before I continue, I realize I left you hanging on the answer Valient Thor gave to Dr. Frank Stranges. The name was Lyndon Johnson. When Dr. Stranges called Bobby Kennedy, he again showed up at Frank's home. When Frank gave him the name, he replied, "I thought so, but just wanted it confirmed." Many investigators have uncovered a lot of evidence that Kennedy was killed because he wanted to reveal the reverse-engineered alien technology, and use it to reach the moon. He and LBJ had argued this point, along with von Braun. It was a very heated argument, two on one, with Kennedy standing alone. Jack Kennedy had been read into the alien presence in 1945, by William Forrestal. They were friends, and Kennedy worked with him for a while. Forrestal was talking about this issue to numerous people. He was then considered a threat to the secrecy and committed to Bethesda Naval Hospital. They claimed he was suffering from a mental breakdown. Everyone, including his family and friends, knew this was untrue. e was then accused of having mental issuesWhen Forrestal was in the hospital, no one was allowed to visit him, not even his own brother. However, members of MJ-12 did visit him. Lyndon Johnson was not a member of Majestic Twelve but worked with them. He was the last person to visit Forrestal before he was pushed from the sixteenth-floor window. I do not think we will ever learn the whole truth, but it is now accepted as fact that he was murdered. e was the lastHe was visited

Bobby Kennedy was shot and killed in 1968, and Dr. Stranges died in 2008. I can tell you this, having done a tremendous amount of due diligence on the JFK assassination, regardless of who was behind it, our country was forever changed. We have been at war since that time. This is because the military industrial complex gained power, a lot of power. In his last speech to Congress, in January of 1961, President Eisenhower warned us of the threat of this group. He said this power, whether sought or unsought, by the military industrial complex posed a serious threat to our future. They have, in large part, had control over the UFOs and the reverse engineering that has been taking place since the 1940s. In addition, we have been at war since the early 1960s.

I have heard insiders swear that Eisenhower had a secret meeting with a race of ETs in 1954. This took place at Edwards Air Force Base. I was told that he was frustrated with the MJ-12 group and what they were doing. Following this meeting, he started the "secret space force" that has existed since that time. However, I never believed it. I felt this was too early in the reverse engineering for this to occur. Then I discovered this was not from ET technology but our own. To build a spacecraft, you need antigravity and a lot of energy. Nichola Tesla and T. Townsend Brown were working on zero-point energy and antigravity, respectively, as far back as the 1920s. Although Tesla died in 1943, other scientists continued and, by October of 1954, had perfected both zero-point energy and antigravity technology. Think about what this means! We should have had free clean energy, antigravity cars, and a clean environment since 1954. Instead, we are running on eighteenth-century technology.

The late Clifford Stone stated he had discovered government documents that stated the following: a group of scientists and engineers had a plan to put a man on the moon by 1960. This same plan called for a moon base by 1963. What is interesting is this plan was developed before NASA was formed. I had heard several years ago that there was a parallel space program running concurrent with the Apollo missions. President Kennedy knew about this, and so did Astronaut Gus Grissom. Gus was one of the original Mercury astronauts and a veteran in the space agency. He died in January 1967 in the Apollo 1 fire, along with Ed White and Roger Chaffee. In the weeks leading up to the fire, Gus was talking, very critical of the Apollo spacecraft. He even hung a lemon on it and said, "Somebody is going to die." I heard he did not have much of a filter, saying what he believed. Supposably, he was telling people we had already put men on the moon and we had far better technology than was shown publicly. He said he and the other astronauts were test dummies, span in a can. Did these comments get him killed? To this day, there are still unanswered questions about that fire. I certainly do not know what occurred, but we do know those in charge would stop at nothing to maintain this secrecy. The three families of the astronauts tried for years to get answers on exactly what happened, to no avail. This is where the acronym for NASA—"Never a Straight Answer"—originated from.

# 29

## DR. VON BRAUN'S PROPHECY AND DEATHBED WARNINGS

Most Americans have heard of Dr. Wernher von Braun, the German rocket scientist who is credited with getting us to the moon. In the years leading up to his death, he was meeting with a female executive from Fairchild Industries, an aerospace company. Her name is Carol Rosen. She became his spokesperson. He told her, over and over again, of what was going on behind the scenes. He said first, we had the Soviets as the enemy, which was happening at that time. He then said we would be fighting terrorists, which we sure did for years. Next it would be renegade countries. We have North Korea, Iraq, and Iran. He then told her the last card they would play would be the alien threat. She said he kept repeating again and again, "It is all a lie." He begged her never to forget this: it is all a lie. This was back in the late 1970s, and it has all come true. During Trump's presidency, he announced the formation of a new branch of the military, the space force. I ask you to now consider this: no governmental agency will openly admit the fact we are not alone in the universe. If they do not know about alien races visiting Earth, then why do we need a space force? Everything I write about in this book is all connected. There have been many governmental reports that have announced that UFOs pose no threat to our national security. They never once said they do not exist. I have followed this story for several decades; heard of countless crashes, encounters, and sightings; and not once have I heard of a hostile act committed by any of them. We have fired on them many times, but they have not fired back. Yet we have been led to believe they are a threat. This has been done by Hollywood numerous times, more recently in the news. The 2017 *New York Times* report was about a group called ATIP, Advanced "Threat" Identification Program. The operative word is always *threat*, in one context or another. Today, all those in the loop will tell you we have been visited for thousands of years. Humans fear anything and everything they do not understand. If they have the technology to travel many light-years to get here, can appear and disappear at will, I ask: How can any human be so arrogant as to think that we could defend ourselves against them? If they were here to destroy us, they would have done so long ago and could do so with the push of a button. Everything von Braun and President Eisenhower warned us about has come true. I wonder this: Is anyone in the media paying attention? You will notice as you read that I repeat some things again and again. This is intentional. I am trying to awaken as many people as possible and demonstrate that these things are all connected.

# 30

## APOLLO MOON MISSIONS

I grew up during the time of our first NASA missions into space. I have clear memories of the Mercury Program. I wanted to be an astronaut, like every kid in those days. From Alan Shepard to Neil Armstrong, they were my heroes. I followed the launch of every mission in amazement. We were all good patriots and believed everything NASA told us. I remember watching as Neil Armstrong took the first step onto the surface of the moon. I was home from college and saw this with my dad. For years, I had no reason to question anything I saw. Over the past twenty-five years, a lot of information has begun to leak out. I now know that things were not as they appeared. People now say that NASA is an acronym for "Never a Straight Answer." For example, when Apollo 11 flew, and their lunar lander named Eagle made contact, both Armstrong and Aldrin looked out and saw six alien spacecraft parked along the edge of the crater. The story was that the voice transmissions were filtered, delayed, for the public. There were HAM radio operators that heard everything, in real time. I never knew if there was any truth in this because no proof was ever presented, at least that I am aware of. Over the years, these stories began to leak out from former NASA employees swearing this was true.

The man I mentioned earlier, William Thompkins, had worked on the Apollo program for four years, initially at Douglas Aircraft, then at North American. He was at TRW, in July 1969, when Armstrong and Aldrin landed. He was directed to go to an off-site location to watch the landing. He saw and heard everything. He confirmed the alien craft parked along the crater. He was a good artist and even drew pictures of the craft. He said there were Reptilian beings standing alongside them. He also spoke of the communication from the astronauts, after they had flown around the dark side of the moon. He stated they had seen buildings being constructed. They were amazed that from one lunar pass to the next, these building were going up a hundred feet. It is now clear this was no surprise to NASA. Before any manned missions to the moon, NASA had sent small robotic craft around the moon, taking pictures. There were seven of these, and at least one landed. They had to select landing sites, and needed to know whether the surface of the moon could withstand the weight of the lunar landers and astronauts. A man named Karl Wolf has spoken publicly on several occasions about being called to go to the NSA (National Security Agency) to work on some equipment. He was then in the military. While there, a young man said to him, "Oh, by the way, we have found bases on the back side of the moon." He then pulled out several mosaics to show him. Karl described what he saw: huge towers, lights, and mushroom- and cone-shaped buildings. Karl became frightened because he knew this fellow should not be showing him these pictures. NASA officials had to know about this, long before our first missions to the moon. If not, then why would they have had Armstrong and Aldrin set out a seismograph during the very first moon landing? Who and why did they think of doing this? When the ascent stage lifted off and did their rendezvous with the mother ship, they released it to fall back onto the surface of the moon. When it hit, the moon rang like a bell for over an hour. On Apollo 17, the final mission, they had placed small rockets on the lunar lander to drive it back into the moon surface. The moon rang like a bell for three days. In addition, when they examined the craters on the moon, regardless of how large they were, the depths were all shallow. One does not need to be a rocket scientist to understand the moon is hollow and is made from something other than soil and rock. If you go to USGS.gov (US Geological Society), they have pictures of ground-penetrating radar of the moon. They show things that appear to be support beams, and a lot of them. This certainly answered my questions.

I realize that if this is new to you, it may be difficult to believe. What I am telling you is based not only in truth but has also been confirmed by many scientists: *our moon is not what we have believed it to be.* I do not know what it is. I have seen many photos of strange things on the surface. For example, there is the giant arch, many times larger than the Saint Louis arch. Then there is the tower, something that looks like a giant cannon, lights, and colors. It is clear these things are not natural. We were told by the Apollo 8 crew, the first mission to the moon in December 1968, that the moon was gray, with no color. Jose Escamilla did a documentary called *Moon Rising*, the greatest story ever denied. He shows many photos of a moon full of color, and evidence of construction taking place. Then there is the shape of the moon. It is a perfect circle and placed at the precise distance to see the complete lunar and solar eclipse. There is no other moon in our solar system like it. Even with the Hubble telescope, they have seen no moon in our galaxy like it. When the Apollo missions returned with hundreds of pounds of rock, geologists discovered there was a five-hundred-million-year difference in the age of the moon rocks and those on Earth. So there goes the collision theory on how it was created. The list of anomalies goes on and on. Later, I will talk about the secret space program and give you more details. The bottom line is that most researchers believe the moon is occupied. Why did we not go back? David Adair talks about this. NASA says they have already explored the moon. David points out that if you add up the combined area of all six moon landings, including the area covered by the rovers, it would equal an area the size of the Mall of America and its parking lots in Minneapolis. This does not include the dark side of the moon. We have not explored 5 percent. Oh, I forgot to point out the fact that our moon is caught in a tidal lock, meaning it does not spin. This is why we never see the dark side. There is something going on with the moon. Every researcher, astronomer, and all who have looked at the facts are talking about it. They know it is mostly hollow. This is simply because they did the math. We know the size and mass. It is approximately thirty-six hundred miles across the face, plus the back side. Some scientist estimated the depth of the surface is five hundred miles. Even if this is true, that still leaves two thousand miles of empty space inside. There are several other reports that say the depth is only fifteen to twenty miles thick. We see the moon from Earth, and it appears small, but it is a large structure. What I do not understand is why this is all a big secret. Why would NASA not tell us the truth? I would love to know the truth as to why we did not return. If it is an artificial structure, a spacecraft, and it is inhabited, it has been postulated they threatened to leave if we came back. If it was not there, it would mess us up bad. The moon controls the tides, the jet stream, and even the polar axis of Earth. Most life on Earth would cease to exist. I am convinced of one thing: there are people who know the truth, and they are walking among us today. The late William Thompkins stated that the moon is a regional space station for this part of our galaxy. Perhaps it is. I do not know.

# 31

## THE AGARTHAN NETWORK

N ow, instead of looking up, I would like to take you down inside the earth. It is now widely known that we have many deep underground military bases, called DUMBs. Places such as the infamous Area 51 are almost completely underground. But this is just the beginning. National labs such as Los Alamos, Sandia Labs, and many others are located deep underground. This is where the deep, dark special-access projects and all the reverse engineering has taken place, and still is taking place. One of the things William Thompkins was most proud of was his work in designing many of these facilities. I saw him being interviewed prior to his death in 2017. He was well into his nineties. It is not so hard to believe we have underground bases, but there is much more. He described tunnels that connect military bases nationwide, with trains running through them. These trains, which I have heard called mag-lift trains, are extremely fast. They go from coast to coast and even up to Nova Scotia. Thompkins described how these were built. He said we have equipment that can drill these tunnels at a rate of two miles per hour. Furthermore, it grounds the material down to microscopic size. Because it is then a crystalline substance, they spray it over the walls, electrically exciting it, and you then have a lighted tunnel. David Adair spoke of being taken to Area 51 many years ago, deep underground, and spoke of how everything was illuminated but he could not see any light source. There are people working in these facilities that have no idea where they are. For example, there have been, and probably still are, scientists living in LA, working at Area 51. They enter a building in LA, take an elevator down, and board a train, and in a matter of minutes, the train stops. They get off, take an elevator up, and are deep inside Area 51. They have no idea of their location and therefore cannot tell anyone where their lab is located. William Thompkins also spoke of huge underground waterways. He said there is an entrance in the San Diego area, where our submarines can enter and go as far as Utah. People have seen submarines there. I believe this may be true, but I have also heard these waterways go through, underneath, the entire country, coast to coast. There is a submarine base in Hawthorne, Nevada. It has been seen by many individuals.

What I now reveal may shock many readers but will certainly surprise most. It sure did me. I first tell you that I have cross-referenced this information through multiple sources. We have all heard stories of the hollow earth. There have been movies made about it. First, the earth is not hollow, but it is honeycombed. There are many giant pockets under the earth's crust worldwide. Some of these pockets are huge, like the size of some states. There is a network of these pockets, said to be eight to twenty miles below the surface, called the Agarthan Network. Some of these pockets are inhabited by various species. The Hopi Indians have stories about the time of the great flood. They were taken down by what they called "the ant people." When we lived in Arizona, I saw petroglyphs on cavern walls, depicting these huge ant people. Many of the native American tribes of the Southwest have oral history that states they originated from under the earth's surface. They also have cave art depicting this. There is another species known as the "Raptors." No one knows their origin, but some think they may have been left over from the dinosaurs. There is yet another species that looks human, like the Nordic ET race. Tall, blond people that are highly advanced. I have heard they have entire civilizations down there, cities, with their own breathable atmosphere and light source. They refer to us as the "stinky surface dwellers." Many researchers believe these tall whites may have been remnants of the Atlantis culture, which disappeared thousands of years ago. There are others living down there, together but separate. Each species has their own areas. My question initially was this: If this is true, then why would they choose to live down there as opposed to joining us on the surface? I have also heard this is a common practice on other planets in the Milky Way galaxy. The answers I found as to why are as follows: some may have been forced underground during catastrophic events, such as the great flood or during the last Ice Age. When all was clear on the surface, they decided to remain there, to live full lives. They realized it is much safer. Consider that they are not subjected to hurricanes, tornadoes, earthquakes, or any weather event that destroys lives and property. They are also free from enemy attacks.

For years, there have been reports of unidentified submergible objects, USOs. They have been seen many times by navy surface ships but frequently by our submarines. A retired navy admiral who was a nuclear submarine captain for over twenty years was asked about whether he had seen USOs. HHe replied there had been too many to count. The most intriguing story he shared was of being in the Indian Ocean, near Antarctica, at their maximum depth. He said they had portals, tiny windows, down in the torpedo storage area. One day he was called by a sailor working in this area who said, "Sir, you had better come down here." He and his first officer proceeded to the lower level of the submarine. They had to crawl through a tight space to look out through these portals. He said they were stunned at what they saw. Several thousand feet below their depth, on the ocean floor, they saw a city the size of Manhattan, with buildings and lights everywhere. They could not believe what they were seeing and began asking each other, "What are you seeing?" All were seeing the same thing. Everyone knew these USOs had to be going somewhere, so they concluded this was one of their bases. Other people who have been in the honeycomb pockets have stated there are space ports down there, and many huge tunnels connecting these pockets. I admit when I first heard of this, I thought, "No way could this be true." However, I have since learned, from multiple sources of highly credible individuals, the same basic story. I am now convinced there is truth here. One thing has become true to me: the ETs are all around us, in the air, in the oceans, and under the surface of the earth. Our submarines have been reporting USOs since the 1950s. They report encounters with huge underwater craft, moving at lightning speeds. It has become clear many are accessing portals to these underground caverns. It all adds up!

I am aware there will be some readers who will reject what I have written. I understand much of this is difficult to accept. I did not arrive at my conclusions overnight. I was a huge skeptic but was very curious. I had seen pictures of lights and heard stories for years Then I began doing research, and this is when I went down the rabbit hole. I had no idea what I was getting into. I consider myself a seeker of truth. To find the truth, I needed solid evidence and from people deep inside. I found so much evidence, I was, and continue to be, blown away. In fact, there is so much evidence that what you read here does not constitute more than 1 percent of what I have learned. In fact, the more I have learned, the more I realize I know nothing. Frankly, it seems that no one person knows the entire story. From the beginning of the cover-up, in the 1940s, the secrecy has been so well structured and compartmentalized that no one person could know the big picture. There have been tens of thousands of people working on pieces of the back engineering. Yet each scientist, engineer, and medical professional only knows their job. They are not allowed to ask any questions whatsoever. To do so might very well get you killed. Emery Smith, who worked in the deep underground special access projects at both Sandia Labs and at Los Alamos, has described this in detail. In the beginning, virtually all this information was in the hands of the military. However, from what I have learned, the navy had recovered a craft from the "Battle of LA" and began their own reverse engineering in 1942. In 1947, the air force got their hands on crashed alien craft. Earlier, I told you of two crashes in New Mexico. However, the famed journalist Linda Moulton Howell got her hands on some MJ-12 documents that said there were three crashes. There were the two I mentioned earlier but another near the White Sands test area. It can become very confusing trying to get to the truth. Regardless of whether there were two or three, it remains that our air force got possession of alien vehicles. They were soon transported to Wright-Patterson AFB in Dayton, Ohio. Later, they were moved to Area 51, which I recently learned was then owned by the CIA. For over fifty years, our government denied the existence of Area 51, just as they did with the NSA and the NRO. In 1969, the air forces project Blue Book ended. Blue Book was established, we were told, to investigate the countless numbers of sightings and provide explanations. Their real mission was to explain them away, with weather balloon and swamp gas stories. What we were never told was that Blue Book not only operated domestically but also worldwide. This is a worldwide phenomenon. Dr. J. Allan Hynick was the lead scientific adviser for Blue Book. During his years there, he became a true believer. After he left Blue Book, he became a noted researcher and a highly acclaimed expert on the subject. He never lived down the "swamp gas" explanation he gave. Following Blue Book, the newly formed DIA took over, the Defense Intelligence Agency. The story we were told was the air force no longer investigated UFOs. In fact, they never stopped. All that changed was that their agents then sent all their reports to the DIA, who then sent everything to the CIA office of scientific intelligence.

# 32

## REVERSE ENGINEERING

In 1997, Lieutenant Colonel Philip Corso published a book called *The Day after Roswell.* Corso had served during WWII. In the early 1960s, he was put in charge of what some refer to as "the Weird Desk" at the Pentagon. He was handed many pieces of material from the crashed UFOs. He was ordered to take each piece to the appropriate industry that would have expertise in the respective area. His desk was formally known as the "Foreign Technology Desk." The deal with each industry was that they took the patents and made as much money as they wanted from them, but then funnel it back to the military for their competitive edge. He named many technologies we have access to today that came directly from reverse-engineered technology. Among these are night vision; printed circuit boards, which led to the first transistor radio, which led to computer chips; and even the bulletproof vest. The list goes on and on. After his book came out, it created quite a stir. He was ridiculed and threatened, as was his family. He died a couple years later. Before his death, his son said he told his family he regretted writing the book, not because any of it was untrue but because he hated to leave his family with this burden. He was being sued. Since his death, he has been vindicated by so many insiders. Several generals have stated that everything he wrote was true and much more. Even industrial executives have verified the truth and accuracy of his story. I ask you to consider this fact: If this is not true, then how do you explain the fact that we have come further technologically in the past sixty years than in the entire known history of humankind? This is just the technology publicly known. The truth is that we have technology today in the secret-access projects that is hundreds and probably thousands of years ahead. According to insiders from the special-access projects, this is technology we cannot even imagine. We went from horse and buggy to the moon almost overnight. In December of 1968, Apollo 8 traveled to the moon, circled it ten times, took the first photos of planet Earth, and returned safely to the earth. This was our first mission to the moon, and it was sixty-five years to the month from the first flight of the Wright brothers. At the time of the first airplane flight, many Americans were still getting around by horse and buggy. How could any civilization get that far and that fast? The answer is simple! We cheated; we had help. Again, the question is why have we been kept in the dark. They had to know the truth would eventually come out. When the internet came along, as well as the fact that everyone has a smartphone with a camera, disclosure became an inevitability.

I will give you more details on reverse engineering later. I am not fabricating anything contained in these pages. Every piece of information is in the public domain. You simply must know where to look.

# 33

## DISCLOSURE
## THROUGH MOVIES

I recently learned the CIA has a department dedicated exclusively to working with our news media and Hollywood. They control much of what we hear and view. We have been getting disclosure for years, especially in movies. The producers and directors have been given details on material to include or not to avoid.

In the 1960s, we have TV shows such as *Star Trek*. This helped to expand human consciousness and got us to thinking in the right direction. Much of the technology on *Star Trek*, which was then considered science fiction, has now been proven scientific reality. This gave rise to a new phrase: "Today's science fiction is tomorrow's scientific fact." In the second half of the '70s, we had the movie *Close Encounters of the Third Kind*. What we did not know at the time was that much of the content of that movie was based on fact and true events. There was an alien landing but not in Wyoming. It was at Holloman Air Force Base in New Mexico. I have been told there are videos, seen by several US presidents, of this event. Like in the movie, an alien craft landed, and ETs stepped out. Several of the characters in the movie were based on real people, like Dr. Jacque Valle, a world-renowned UFO researcher. Dr. J. Allen Hynick, who was the lead scientific adviser for Project Blue Book, is seen in a cameo part in the movie. He acted as an adviser on the production. He also wrote the story. They used sound and mathematics to communicate with the aliens, which is all based in truth. Sound and math are used universally to communicate. We know that every geometric shape, a square, a triangle, a cone, has a corresponding sound behind it. Yes, Hollywood took their dramatic licenses, but much of that movie is based in truth. Then came the *Star Wars* series of movies. I think I have watched every one of them. I remember wondering, even back then, what kind of mind could create all the many details. Only within the past year, I was speaking to one of my best friends, who has been involved in ufology for years. He told me the story of Riley Martin, who was an uneducated man from Arkansas. Riley had been abducted by an ET race of mostly "gray" aliens. However, this was not the typical abduction we hear about so often.

He reported being abducted many times and traveling with them, throughout the Milky Way. He stated they were interested in knowing about us and asked him many questions. They even asked him about his religious beliefs, which really surprised him. He realized that God was as much a mystery to them as to us. He said they shared stories of galactic wars that had taken place between light and dark forces. I am not sure how long this persisted, but it had to be over a relatively long period. Anyway, he returned and began telling people the stories and what they had shared with him. His story became public. Then came the *Star Wars* movies, much of which included his same stories. My friend told me that Riley was furious, because he never received a dime in royalties. Do you remember in the movie when the Death Star destroyed an entire planet? Well, there is a lot of evidence that this did happen in our own solar system. If you look through a telescope, there is an asteroid belt between Mars and Saturn. In fact, researchers of ancient civilizations have postulated that it was a water planet. When it was destroyed, much of the water, which turned to ice, hit the earth, as well as some pieces of the asteroids. This, they say, may have created the great flood and the last Ice Age. I must say, this sounds far-fetched, but the fact remains, the asteroid belt does exist. Where else could it have originated from? Lastly, our astronomers and individuals who claim to have served in the "secret space program," have stated they have seen one of these "giant Death Stars," or something very similar. The truth can certainly be stranger than fiction. I have no proof of any of this and am not sure what to believe. I do see that many of the dots connect. Whatever is real, it makes an interesting story.

There is another piece of history to the *Star Wars* story. Researcher Billy Carson has studied thousands of ancient texts. The Egyptian god Thoth spoke of star wars, which were battles between light and darkness. Thoth spoke of the "force" running through all of us, which we now know is the fractal light energy from our Creator. He then spoke of the "dark brothers," which I understood as being the dark forces. They have attacked every thriving civilization, infusing the people with ego, which is followed by greed and the pursuit of power. The dark brothers have destroyed civilizations throughout the universe. I thought, "Wow, this sounds familiar." He also said the Jedi knights were real, and still exist, fighting the dark forces. They originated from the Orion star system. If this is true, we sure need them here today.

# 34

## SECRECY AND SPECIAL-ACCESS PROJECTS

Most everyone that investigates this phenomenon eventually asks the same questions and arrives at the same conclusions. One of the big questions is: Why were we not told the truth? The answer to this is not simple. There have been many players, all with different agendas. The government felt they could not tell us because no one really understood the phenomenon. How could they tell us that we were being visited, but had no idea what their motives were? In addition, they could fly over our military bases, our nuclear missile silos, shut them down at will, and we could do nothing about it. Our fastest jets could not even get close to them. Earlier, I spoke of the flyover of several UFOs in 1952, which took place on two consecutive weekends. Following the first weekend, President Truman was going to order our air force to shoot them down, should they return. I ask you to think about this. The UFOs had shown no aggression and did nothing to hurt or harm anyone. They had simply entered our airspace. There is documentation that during the week following the first flyover, Dr. Albert Einstein showed up at the White House, having heard of Truman's order to shoot them down. Basically, he told Truman that if these people could travel millions of miles to get here, they would be able to take care of themselves. He said, "Please do not start something you cannot finish." Truman then rescinded the shoot-down order. They concluded that telling the public would destabilize the country, scare people to death, and change nothing. They were, and still are today, very concerned about the impact it would have on religions. Still, there were many others, namely the military industrial complex, that were solely motivated by greed. They knew they could make billions of dollars from the reverse engineering. In addition, many others believe the ETs themselves are behind the secrecy. It is now an accepted fact that they have been visiting Earth for at least thousands of years. They have mostly operated by stealth but have certainly shown themselves many times. I am personally convinced they are waiting on us to evolve spiritually and in consciousness. In fact, many contactees have reported being told this very thing. Recently, I watched an interview with a Canadian man named Grant Cameron. He is known as the "document guy." He has researched the UFO phenomenon since 1975 and collected tens of thousands of government documents on the subject. He discovered many documents from presidential libraries, from Truman to the present. More recently, following the death of Dr. Edgar Mitchell, the sixth man to walk on the moon and a major player in the UFO community, Cameron gained access to many of his files. Grant has written several books on this topic and revealed many classified documents. If you are still a nonbeliever in this subject, I encourage you to read his books, which are full of proof, in black and white. At the end of the interview, he made a statement that I completely agree with. He first pointed out that no one really understands this phenomenon. Most have seen it, only in terms of the technology, which is hundreds, even thousands, of years beyond ours. Many others have reacted only out of fear. However, he believes that when we are finally shown the truth, it is going to be a lot more spiritual, more about consciousness than about the "nuts and bolts" of technology. Not only do I agree with him, but this is one reason I am writing this book. I am sure many readers have been wondering why I began the first chapters discussing spirituality, the need for us to awaken to who we truly are, and then begin writing about ETs and UFOs. The reason is simple. It is all connected. The aliens know things we do not. They are highly evolved beings and understand the fact that we are all part of the same being, of the same Creator, which I call God and they refer to as Source.

# 35

## DIRECT CONTACT
## WITH ALIEN SPECIES

I have watched many interviews of people who claim to have had direct contact with alien beings. Some communicated verbally but mostly telepathically. They have reported receiving a download of love, which was beyond words. Every one of the humans who has experienced these meetings seems to take offense when others see them as a threat. The late Clifford Stone, who was an "interfacer" for the military at crash scenes, was selected because he had telepathic skills. He said, to his dying breath, they were wonderful souls. Furthermore, they had families and likes and dislikes, and were full of empathy and compassion. Emery Smith worked alongside many species in the special-access projects in surgical suites.

He, too, reported how precious life was to them. In contrast to these individuals, we have many military and intelligence people who see all ETs as a threat. I find these perspectives totally fear based. If you ask these same people to provide an example of how they have demonstrated hostility, most cannot name even one incident. This is just another example of humans fearing anything they do not understand. Earlier in this book, I spoke of how we humans are living in a 3D reality, but must evolve into the fourth and fifth harmonic density. Once this occurs, we will then realize we are all the same consciousness, one with our Creator. Once we evolve, wars will cease, and crime will drop like a rock. We will live in a love-based frequency versus a fear-based one. Along with these attributes, we will grow in compassion, in empathy, and in happiness. Now consider this: most all the extraterrestrial civilizations evolved beyond the third density, even beyond the fourth, hundreds or thousands of years ago. When the first crashes of ET craft occurred in the 1940s, I find it very unfortunate that it was our military people that became involved. Then the military industrial complex came into the picture. Sadly, the only thing they cared about was the technology, meaning money. I have heard again and again that the ETs gave us a lot of technology to benefit humanity. Instead, it was kept secret and turned into weapons. However, our top physicists and scientists could not understand the technology, especially the propulsion systems. Most of them were so arrogant, thinking they knew everything; it was years before they began to figure it out. For example, they could not understand the materials they were made from. They said things like, "We know every element in the universe, which is on the periodic table." Not one of them had ever been off this planet and had no clue what was in the universe. Secondly, they were trying to use Newtonian physics to understand it. Following several years of futile attempts, they finally realized these craft were built with a different physics and they had to go back to elementary school and start all over again. They had several different craft, from different ET races, and each had its own unique technology. They used different methods of propulsion. Over the years, with the help of the ETs themselves, they figured it out. By 1993, Ben Rich, who was director of Lockhead Skunkworks, was delivering a talk to a group of students at the UCLA School of Engineering. He told them: "We now have the technology to take ET home." With many of the students present, his comment went in one ear and out the other. There were other alumni present whom his statement was not wasted on. One of them was a man who had been obsessed with this technology. Following the talk, this man approached Ben Rich and asked him one question: How is it possible for these craft to fly through space, traveling light-years in a relatively short period of time? To his surprise, Ben replied with a question. He asked: How does ESP work?

The man said he was caught off guard but answered with the only thing he could think of. He said, "All points in space and time are connected?" Ben Rich replied, "There, you have it," and left the building. I have since learned these craft are flown by conscious-assisted technology. Some of these craft are biological. Inside these spaceships, there are no controls. There are indentations where they place their hands and fingers. The craft are then flown with their minds. It is all about consciousness, which is another reason we must awaken and evolve. My first thought was "Try reverse engineering that!" I am now told our scientists have managed to figure it out. For years, many of our smartest and brightest refused to believe these ETs were visiting us because they could not comprehend how it was possible to traverse distances that would require a million years, using our best linear technology. It turns out they were right except these alien beings do not travel in a straight line. They use different methods, wormholes, and portals and fold the space in front of them, pull it to them, and jump over it. David Adair describes it as like rolling a burrito. The craft is in the middle, where the filling of the burrito would be, then they roll the space around them. They then jump from one layer to the next. They only travel a very short distance but are jumping over entire quadrants of space. David has developed a device he calls "an electromagnetic containment device." It can contain the fury of an "H-bomb."e H He refers to it as a mini-wormhole.

He said he just followed the math but pointed out he was not talking about adding and dividing numbers. This is quantum differential mechanics. Once he built the containment device and got it stabilized, the math led him to another set of algorithms, which gave him what he calls an "inertia dampener." This is another field around his device and craft. Many people have reported seeing these UFOs fly into our atmosphere at five thousand miles per hour and make ninety-degree turns, which would turn the occupants into soup due to the G-forces. This would happen using our known technology. However, with this inertia dampener, the occupants are inside their own field and feel *nothing*! David said this is how they are doing it, or it is something very similar. Makes sense to me.

# 36

## WORMHOLE / JUMP
## GATE TRAVEL

Now I go back to the wormhole concept. Most of us are not aware of this, but if you have been reading this book for an hour, you, your home, the town you live in, and the entire planet have traveled through space one hundred thousand miles. This is a fact. Every year, there are thousands of people who disappear. People have witnessed this. For example, a man and a woman are walking through a park, side by side, and in the blink of an eye, one of them vanishes, never to be seen again. Where did they go? It is postulated that they passed through a tiny wormhole. David Adair shared a story that he was directly involved in, as an investigator. A woman and her young daughter were living in what he referred to as a poor house but a stand-alone home in Chicago. Suddenly, a bright light appeared. The little girl got excited, said, "Look, Mommy," and went toward the light. The mother went after her, as any mother would do. The next second, the same light appeared in a dorm room at the University of Toronto, Canada, and there stood the woman and her little girl, wearing nothing but their jammies. The students sitting in the room studying were freaked out and called the police. Immediately, the authorities tracked every airplane flight, train, and bus to try and find out how they got there. They found nothing. At the same time back in Chicago, authorities canvassed her neighborhood. They found neighbors who said they had seen her within the hour. One neighbor said, "I just spoke with her, and she was inside her house." Explain that! David said when he went to investigate, the entire house was gone, just a slab. The spot was fenced off with a sign that read, "Property of the US Government." They concluded she had passed through a wormhole, but they have no way of knowing for sure.

What is a wormhole? How are they formed? I had heard about them for years but knew very little. David Adair just may be the most intelligent person I have ever listened to. Yet he has a manner of speaking and explaining things that even I can understand. To explain how a wormhole is formed, we begin with a sun. Our star is a medium yellow sun and is five hundred thousand miles across. A sun is like thousands of H-bombs going off at the same time. They explode outward but are pulled back in by gravity, until this process is stabilized. Then, we have a sun we see daily. Now we know that in time, suns burn out. This occurs because they run out of fuel. But the gravity always wins. It pulls and shrinks all the mass to a smaller and smaller object. It takes it down to the size of a basketball. However, it still weighs the same as it did at five hundred thousand miles across. But it is not through. It continues to shrink down to a smaller and smaller size, to a grain of sand, but still maintains the same weight. Finally, it shrinks below the size of a tachyon particle, and a singularity is formed, with an event horizon, that can suck anything inside, another sun, a planet, etcetera. It is strongly believed the aliens are traveling through wormholes. What I do not get is how they even find them, nor how they enter them. I have also heard from several sources that we are now traveling through portal technology, or jump gates. I am sure we got this from the ETs. They explained this as walking up to a doorway, stepping through, and you might come out on the other side of your city, in the inner earth, on the moon, or on another planet. They said you might only take a couple of steps to get to the other side. The only physical effect is in the inner ear. You may feel a little disoriented for a few minutes, especially the first time you do this. They now have technology to manufacture a man-made wormhole or jump gate.

I recently learned that we now have satellites that can see through the earth. They can also pick up both light and energy spectrums throughout the land and sea. They are no using them commercially to see into the walls of homes and investigate what type of termites many be infesting. This is how they discovered electromagnetic signatures on land, and deep in the oceans, that reflect portals or jump gates. They have now discovered another way our alien visitors are coming and going. I had told you of the advanced technology to build the tunnels and underground bases. When the discovered these portals in some of the deepest parts of our oceans, like the Mariana Trench, they wanted to observe. So they dug deep under the ground, from the states, through the rock under the ocean floor. When they reached the area of a portal, they used a high-powered energy device to displace the water over a large area. They then constructed a "dome" of a clear, transparent, material. It is several feet thick and was made from reverse-engineered material. From these facilities—and there are now many—they observe the craft entering and departing. They are also studying life forms, like Aquafarians, what we know of as "mermaids." They look like us from the waist up but have fins and breathe through gills. I heard this from a man who went to one of these facilities to work on one of these beings, in an operating room filled with salt water. There are now plans to reveal this information to the public soon.

I also learned that we now have access to some of these portals, mostly from reverse-engineered ET technology. This did not surprise me, but here is what did: we have been sending teams of scientists and highly trained individuals on missions through these portals. Some go to inner earth pockets, but most go to other planets. These missions are very dangerous, and several have died because the technology is not perfected. They train for months, and once they step through, they only stay a few minutes. This is mostly because the portals only remain open for short periods. They can close, and people may not be able to return. While there, they collect samples of everything. For example, on one mission, the collected a leaf that was four feet wide. They later discovered it was bulletproof. Naturally, the back-engineering began instantly. They are now making new pharmaceuticals from much of what has been collected. This has been going on for over thirty years. The teams are typically military people. This is because if they die, they can tell the family it was in the line of duty. I realize this may be hard to believe. Initially, I was shocked, but this information came from a highly credible source, whom I trust.

# 37

## PUBLIC AWARENESS

In 2001, an event was held at the Washington Press Club called the "Disclosure Project." It was orchestrated by Dr. Steven Greer and by Steven Bassett, or the Paradigm Research Group. They had dozens of government insiders testify, all whom had had firsthand knowledge with the UFO subject. It is important to understand that each of these individuals was risking everything by testifying—their careers, their lives, and the lives of their families. They received no money. Their only motive was because they believed you and I have a right to know the truth. This event lasted four days and was the most watched event in the history of the Press Club. In attendance were current and former members of Congress and many others. Paola Harris, an internationally known field investigative journalist, said she watched the expressions on people's faces as they heard the testimony. She said some were white as sheets, and others sat there with their mouths wide open. I also watched much of it and was blown away. These were unimpeachable witnesses, with impeccable credentials, who testified. You can find it online today or watch Dr. Greer's documentary titled *Unacknowledged*. I have directed many people to watch the documentary. If you still question whether we are alone in the universe after watching it, well, I do not think there is anything left to say.

Unfortunately, the 9/11 attack happened shortly afterward, which overshadowed everything for a long while. However, in 2013, Steven Bassett put together a similar event at the Washington Press Club called the Citizens Hearing on UFOs. He had over forty military people who testified. They gave detailed descriptions of alien visitors over nuclear sites, the fact they either shut them down or permanently destroyed them. Steven Bassett is the only registered lobbyist in Washington on the UFO phenomenon. He has dedicated his life to one cause, what he refers to as lifting the truth embargo. Dr. Steven Greer was a trauma surgeon but gave up his medical practice to devote his time and life to bringing the truth out. He has a second documentary called *CE-5: Close Encounters of the Fifth Kind*. He developed protocols to help us make direct contact with alien races. He has led groups nationwide, and in Europe, in these CE-5 encounters. They have had unbelievable success. You can download his protocols. I need to point out that the success is mostly dependent on the participants coming from an inner place of love. If the ETs sense fear, they back away. He is responsible for shining light on the darkness of this subject for decades. He has personally briefed many members of Congress, the Senate, military officers, and even a former director of the CIA for the Clinton administration. It is important to note that this secret has been so compartmentalized that many of our elected officials, generals, admirals, etcetera do not know any more than the average person on the street. However, this has been changing since 2017. Something has happened that has created a sense of urgency to bring about disclosure. Congress and Senate members have been receiving briefings since that time frame.

The most important thoughts I have had about all these people who have testified is the courage it required for them to share their stories publicly. These are good and decent people, who had been compelled to live in fear, while carrying knowledge they knew should be public. Many were former military. In the military, if a superior gives you an order, you follow it, even though you may totally disagree with it. These were average people, like me and you, who witnessed incredible things. They were told things such as "You did not see anything," "This never happened," and "Should you tell anyone, we will make you disappear." They were threatened in every way imaginable. Furthermore, those in charge of many of these events were operating outside the laws of our country, in secrecy. I am amazed that despite this, they chose to step forward and tell the truth, in public, before cameras and microphones. That requires a level of courage that most of us would say is uncommon valor. In my opinion, they are heroes. Despite this, many are still being ridiculed and threatened. The hope I have is that one day soon, we will finally receive disclosure, and every one of these heroes will be vindicated. In fact, I know that by writing this book, I will be ridiculed by some. I know that one day soon, I, too, will be vindicated, along with so many others.

# 38

---

## PRESIDENTIAL BRIEFINGS
## AND HUMAN FREQUENCIES

---

In the 1980 time frame, there were several significant things that occurred. Ronald Reagan was elected president and took office in January of 1981. There are documents showing that he was fully briefed on the UFO subject by then CIA director Bill Casey. Linda Moulton Howe got copies of this briefing. Others were also present from the NSA and the NRO. Reagan was told of five different alien races that we were in contact with, with one being hostile. He was blown away, even though he was already a believer, having seen a UFO himself. He was informed of many things on this topic, but one was the fact they are here now, walking among us. He became concerned that they might infiltrate our government, including the

White House. He then directed our intelligence agencies to find ways to detect them. We now know that DNA is probably the best way, but keep in mind that DNA test did not come into play for several years following this time. Earlier in this book, I mentioned that we all have a distinct frequency, one that is as unique to us as a fingerprint. I told you there is a piece of technology that can read these frequencies. What I did not tell you was how and why this device came about. It was developed to detect ETs and hybrids. Humans all have a different frequency, but all fall within a certain range. ETs have a much higher range of frequency. We are evolving to these higher frequencies. They also use brain wave activity to detect them. We also know there are many hybrids among us. Estimates say there are at least thousands. There are several of them working in our intelligence agencies. They have gifts and abilities we humans do not possess. I admit this surprised me, but once I had accumulated many facts, it made sense. Richard Doty, a former air force OSI (Office of Special Intelligence) agent, told of two of these, both females, he had uncovered and brought into the OSI.

Many documents surfaced in the 1980s. One provided proof that the M-12 group was real. It still exists today but under a different name. As a reminder, MJ-12 was the above-top-secret group formed to investigate UFOs and to oversee the reverse engineering back in 1947. Many of us can still recall Reagan talking about ETs in many of his speeches. Later in his presidency, he made a speech at the United Nations. To paraphrase, he asked: How fast would all our differences disappear if we were suddenly confronted with an invasion from an alien species? Grant Cameron found his handwritten notes on this speech at the Reagan Library. He had written this himself, as opposed to what normally occurs, with speechwriters constructing everything a president says. Grant found many essays Reagan had written to himself on the subject.

# 39

## THE TWENTY YEARS AND BACK PROGRAM

Several years ago, I heard the story of a man named Randy Cramer. He claims he served off-planet in the secret space force, in what is called the "twenty and back program." He said he was taken at age seventeen, served twenty years, and was then returned fifteen minutes after he left, at the same age. Initially, he had no memory of anything that had happened during his tour of duty. I thought this was the most ridiculous thing I had ever heard of. I got a good laugh out of it, but I never forgot it. The narrator of the program even said he did not know what to make of it. However, he pointed out that Randy had been telling the same story for ten years, with no deviation. If someone is lying, they will always slip up in time. I thought this impossible, but the more I have learned, the more I have come to realize that nothing is impossible. Following the initial program where this story began, I heard nothing more about it for several years. As crazy as it sounded, I found myself thinking about it. I still did not believe it but could not dismiss it either. Earlier, I spoke of William Thompkins and Dr. Robert Wood. Thompkins was a brilliant designer. He had designed many of the deep underground bases for the military. He had also designed complex 39-a and the checkout facility at Cape Canaveral, working with Dr. Wernher von Braun. He had served in a top-secret capacity for the navy in WWII and was navy through and through. Then I saw video of him discussing the fact that he had designed space carriers for the navy. He said they were two, four, and six kilometers in length. He held up copies of his designs. This project was called "Solar Warden." He said they were built and in operation by 1979. This was the beginning of the secret space program, at least by the navy. Dr. Wood said one of the first spacecraft he knew about was a submarine. They had removed the nuclear reactor and replaced it with an antigravity engine and launched it. It was already airtight. Next, Bill Thompkins spoke of the need for personnel. He began describing the twenty and back program. He gave many of the same details offered by Randy Cramer. This got my attention. Then I found a series of interviews with Randy on Gaia TV. They had given him polygraph test, one that is said to be impossible to beat. I am a pretty good judge of character, having been in the people business for over three decades. If he is lying, he sure has me fooled. Furthermore, he would deserve an Academy Award for his performance. To add more credibility, I have seen interviews of three other men. One was Michael Jaco, whom I mentioned earlier. The others were Jason Rice and Corey Good. They had experienced different things, but the core of their stories is almost identical. To add even more credibility to this story, a British citizen named Gary McKinnon hacked into our Department of Defense, looking for information on UFOs. To his surprise, he found a list entitled "Nonterrestrial Officers." After spending dozens of hours watching interviews with these men, none of whom appear to be connected in any way, I reached a crossroads. Did I just laugh it off as crazy, which I initially had done, or did I accept it as factual? Each of them has been polygraphed and placed under hypnosis. With at least two of them, Gaia brought in psychotherapists like Dr. Barbara Lamb, who did regression hypnosis on them. With these two, it not only provided proof of their statements but also helped them to recall even more details of their tours of duty. Some people, including William Thompkins, referred to what happened at the end of the twenty years as a mind wipe. Randy Cramer describes it as being more of memory suppression. He said it took him ten years to get most of his memories back, but twenty years to recover. I can only tell you that I agree with many others that now believe these stories. They are so full of details, there is no way these men could be making this up.

The stories they describe made me feel like I was living in a *Star Wars* movie. There is no way I can even begin to describe it all. If you are interested, go to Gaia TV and watch *Cosmic Disclosure.* I will give you a few details here. The one thing each had in common was first going to a base on the moon called Lunar Operations Command. From there, they went to Mars for more training and experience. All said that life exist throughout our solar system, on every planet, or the moons. From there, they were deployed to other planets outside our solar system. There, they engaged in combat with aggressive species. They provide many details about these battles and the various species they fought. They described advanced weapons, far beyond what our special forces teams are using. These men were serving at different times, over the past forty to fifty years. Randy appears to be the oldest. He now claims to have become the public spokesperson for the marine corps special section. He is speaking at the behest of his general. He is an officer and still active. I will share one story he told. The reason is it provides so much insight about what may be taking place. When he was late in his tour, he was a pilot on a space carrier called the Nautilus. From time to time, they carried ambassadors to attend meetings with ambassadors from other planets. This took place on a giant craft orbiting Jupiter. Although he said this craft is cloaked, our astronomers have seen giant spacecraft around Jupiter. He described it as looking like a giant bell. On the top floor, there was a huge, circular meeting room, which is a mile around. He said it was run by the Galactic Trade Federation, with meeting environments. He was taken along because he was the only pilot on board with infantry experience, as a "just-in-case guy." He pointed out several times that he was never needed for any just-in-case situation. He said each time he was there, it was always at least 75 percent full to completely full. Here is why I tell you this story: there were hundreds of different sentient beings present. He said the smallest species was about eighteen inches tall, and the largest was over fifty feet tall. This tall species looked just like humans. They were from a much larger planet, on a different scale than us. He was told they are a near genetic match to us. He described everything one could imagine. There were species that had evolved from tree frogs, avian, aquatic, and one species that was canine. There were others who breathed other gases, like methane. I began to understand what he meant by meeting environments. He recalled sitting across the table with "people" in a water environment. Some wore environment suits, and others were jump-gated into an aquatic container. He said the biggest problem they had upon arrival was that the mind simply cannot process the visual appearances of all these different species. They would get headaches and had to sit and stare at the floor until the headaches went away. Often, they had to repeat the process a couple of times. Then they could stand up and walk to the area of their meeting.

The purpose of all the meetings was for trade. My mind was already stretched, but now it dawned on me what he was saying. We have agreements, contracts, with many other alien civilizations. The Cabal is making trillions of dollars by selling to many other planets. Think about this: if you have a product to see, and it has a worldwide market of $100 million, by expanding the market to the galaxy, the market becomes a kazillion-dollar market.

In the beginning, it was only the military, specifically the navy, going into space. Today there are elements of most US military, and from governments all over the world. At least the G-20 countries. But that is not all. Industries that have the financial resources and the know-how have their own spacecraft.

One thing I did hear from Randy Cramer that made complete sense is that the two planets, where he was stationed for a short time, had inhabitants that were humanoid and like us. He guessed they were maybe 150 years beyond where we are today. They were democracies but without the political end fighting we have here. Every citizen is encouraged to do what they are most gifted at and love to do. They viewed their citizens as their largest assets. When they heard of the poverty, crime, and class warfare we have, they could not believe it. They saw this as a total waste for a civilization not to make the most out of what their citizens could contribute. They had no problem with a company making a profit, unless they should become greedy, which was very rare. Their mentality was about serving the common good. When everyone does well, business fares even better. They make more money, not less. Crime and violence were almost unheard of. They used clean, free energy and drove antigravity cars. The air was clean, and so was the entire planet. He said he was asked, "Why would we want to make ourselves miserable?" We spend our lives struggling to feed our families and keep a roof over our heads. Our civilization is an inverted one. By this, I mean almost all the wealth and power are at the top of the pyramid. If we look at this from a purely mathematical point of view, this cannot stand. Our civilization will topple under its own weight. Make no mistake: this is not Communism; they are democracies. We must to find a way to create more balance. We will still have wealthy people but not to the extremes. Those at the top either must give up a relatively small amount of their money, or the entire civilization will crumble under their feet and ours. Instead of giving handouts to millions of people, we need to find at least one talent they possess and train them to provide for themselves. By doing this, they, too, will contribute to the whole of civilization. Folks, it is not that complicated, only common sense. There is no need for us to live as we have been, in a state of continuous struggle. This also eliminates worry and fear.

As I said earlier, I initially thought this was nuts. It just sounded too far out. However, over a long period of time, I have connected the dots. I have received confirmation from a wide variety of sources. There is simply too much smoke for no fire to exist. In conclusion, I am now about 95 percent sure this is happening and has been for decades. I am not basing my belief just on what these individuals from the SSP (Secret Space Program) are saying. It is the totality of information, going back to the Eisenhower and Kennedy era. I have heard from so many insiders who have provided pieces of information, from the origins of the plans for a secret space force, to those who have designed the craft, and insiders who have shared details. I again think to myself: if these stories did not sound out of this world, how could I believe them?

# 40

## ABDUCTIONS

It is widely known that aliens have been abducting humans for centuries, at least back to biblical times. The most famous case in our times occurred in 1961 in New Hampshire. This was the Betty and Barney Hill story. While on their way home one night, they were taken aboard a spacecraft. While aboard, Betty asked them where they were from. Telepathically, they downloaded a star map into her brain. A few weeks later, while under hypnosis, she was able to draw it. At the time, none of our astronomers recognized it. In fact, they used this as a means of discrediting the event. Several years later, noted astronomer Carl Segan found the constellation. The earth is moving constantly, and so are all bodies in the universe. It turned out it was in the Zeta Reticulin star system, where the EBENs are from. If I understand correctly, it can only be seen from Earth every few years, at least with the telescopes available at that time. This meant there was no way she could have fabricated her drawing. She was vindicated, and no one has ever been able to discredit the story.

Dr. John Mack, a psychiatrist and Harvard University professor, dedicated much of his career to working with abduction cases. Not only did he receive lots of ridicule, but they also attempted to get him thrown out of the university. He never wavered and stuck to what he knew to be true. In the end, he kept his position. I had heard of so many cases, too many to count, and concluded they were real.

However, it became more real to me when I contacted a person who was abducted several times throughout her life. This phenomenon then became very real to me. Several months ago, I was in conversation with an old and dear friend, whom I had known since childhood. He had experienced a couple of close-up UFO sightings many years ago. He had never told me. Until recently, most people just did not talk about this sort of thing. He spent years in the UFO community, learning everything he could. Anyway, we were talking about abductions. He told me about a relative of his who had been abducted several times. He asked me if I would like to speak with her, as he knew I was conducting research for this book. Of course I jumped at the opportunity. He sent me her name and contact information. Initially, I was a bit hesitant. I do not like to impose on anyone's privacy. After a few days, I sent her a message, explaining who I was. She did not respond right away. I was sure she would call my friend first. She also read my book *Shining Bear*. After a relatively short period of time, a couple of weeks, she called me. Over time, she opened up more and more to me. She has been able to astral project, since she was a kid. For those less informed, this means to leave your physical body and travel anywhere in your light body. Much of her story is very similar to countless others I have listened to. It began when she was around twelve years old. She was taken aboard a craft, and there were gray aliens but also a couple of other species present. The worst part for her is they wiped her memory. She cannot recall many of the details. She is now in her late seventies and has not had a visit from them in four years that she recalls. I had heard many of these stories, but speaking directly to someone who has experienced abductions has shifted my own reality. She and I have become friends and talk often. I think much of the truth will come from people like her. She is now starting to write her own story. She claims I motivated her; regardless, I am very happy she is again confronting this series of events in her life. My hope is that she will recall more details. She only has pieces of many of her encounters. I suspect she may be a hybrid. I confronted her about it, and to my surprise, she did not reject the idea. The reason for my suspicion is that the aliens will follow a hybrid throughout their life, which has been the case with her. There is so much conversation and conjecture as to why they are here and what they want. She strongly feels the answers can be obtained by listening to the abductees. We will likely never get a straight answer from any government agency. I agree with her. However, most of these people have been unwilling to talk, due to the ridicule and harassment. Even she has never really discussed this with anyone outside her family. I may be one of the only outsiders she has described these events to. This has changed a great deal in recent years, with more public discussion on the matter. This ridicule has happened, even with those who have simply reported seeing an alien craft. They have often received this harassment from neighbors, family members, as well as orchestrated ridicule from the government. Many have said they regretted ever saying a word. They say if it occurs again, they will tell no one. I certainly do not blame them. People can be so cruel.

In the first chapters of this book, I spoke of the fact we are coming to the end of a cycle, that we are "shifting." Everything in this book is connected. Earlier this year, I watched some interviews on Gaia TV with a woman named Anjoli. She is a former intelligence officer for the DIA (Defense Intelligence Agency). She had left to become a contractor and moved to California. Once there, she began having contact with alien beings. It is a long story as to how her story unfolded. I will give you the abbreviated version. Eventually, she was taken inside a mountain. There she met with a council, a federation of several races of beings. They shared many things with her, and she is now on a mission to get the word out to the world. Before I get into the specifics, it is important to note this was not her first interface with ETs.

When she was about four years of age, living in Jacksonville, Florida, she was in her bed one night, and the next thing she knew she was aboard a spacecraft, which was hovering over her house. While on board this craft, she encountered several children of different ages and sizes. She was told, "These are your brothers and sisters." They explained that these children did not pass for humans, but she did. She described it as a wonderful experience. The only conclusion to be drawn is that she is a hybrid. She was placed here to help humanity awaken. The awakening is exactly what I have been speaking of. We must awaken to the fact that we are all consciousness, that our physical bodies are just temporary vessels we use to experience, learn, and evolve. I was amazed to hear her describe exactly what I have been talking about.

They told her that the earth is nearing the end of a cycle, that there will be another reset. We know this occurred when we had the great flood. They told her it has happened too many times to count, over the past four billion years. To be honest, this frightened me a little. They told her the poles of Earth will shift, and everything will be turned upside down. To add credibility to this story, our own scientists are saying the same things. This federation is trying to awaken as many people as possible before this takes place. Those that do not awaken may be in trouble. What she described is an event where most human bodies will be wiped out. However, just before this occurs, they will collect all their people and many who have awakened. These people will be returned after the catastrophe ends. She points out, again and again, that this is not the end, but a new beginning. We do not die because we are consciousness. Following this event, we will move into the fourth or fifth harmonic density. I am unclear about what happens to those who fail to awaken, but I got a sense it was not good. I pray I am wrong. They also told her this was never meant to be a permanent situation here on Earth. They referred to it as being an experiment. I have heard this numerous times and from several sources.

One last point she made was that many of us are waiting on the ETs to show up. She said, "No need to wait; they are already here en masse." Many individuals within our government know and have known this for decades. They also know that several of the ET races are placing human hybrids here. This has been known, at least since the early 1980s, and probably longer.

I now tell you about a fact that very few people know about. Emery Smith worked in the labs of the special-access projects for years. He was dissecting tissue from alien beings. This was in the early 1990s, when the use of DNA was becoming pervasive. The genetic labs were looking at the DNA of a variety of alien races, many of which they collected from crash sites or captured. What they discovered was astounding. Although the DNA was significantly different from humans, they found some human DNA in virtually every one. For contrast, they examined the DNA of many humans. They discovered that we all have varying amounts of extraterrestrial DNA within us, but from different alien species. The true hybrids just have higher levels of alien DNA, or enhancements. It became obvious, once again, that we are all connected, but in more ways than in consciousness alone. Some of the ET races are experts in genetics. They have been cloning for eons. We are now doing the same thing. The Chinese are producing clones for abstracting organs for some of their people. Our people say this is crazy because you can 3D-print any organ or body part. We now know that ETs have been tinkering with our DNA for thousands of years. Earlier, I mentioned that our geneticists say we have a lot of "junk DNA." They have not discovered its purpose. Something tells me it is there for a reason. I suspect when the shift occurs, the ETs may activate this portion of our genetics. Everything inside me says this shift is imminent. However, I am still human and cannot help feeling some fear. There is a part of me that wants to reject all of this. Yet most of us sense a change is coming, one we cannot understand. All we can do is make sure we are prepared, both consciously and in mental awareness. Deep down, I feel it will be a good and wonderful shift.

# 41

## ANCIENT CIVILIZATION
## AND TEACHINGS

I am not going to delve into ancient history nor ancient civilizations here. However, oweverHI would be remiss if I do not bring it up. What we have been taught in school, in our history books, is almost all incorrect. Virtually all researchers confirm this. For example, if we are to believe traditional historians, human history began about six thousand years ago. Researchers have found and studied many ancient texts, which are full of information on advanced technology. Examples of these texts are the Sumerian texts from Mesopotamia, the Veda and the Mahabharata text from India, and the teachings of Thoth from ancient Egypt. Our word thought was derived from Thoth. In the Sumerian text, the stories of the Anunnaki appears.

Initially, they thought Anunnaki was one ET race, but they now know the term means "those who came from the stars," or from the heavens. In fact, they consisted of several races. In a museum in Oxford, England, you will find the antediluvian kings list. It gives a list of kings who ruled over Earth for tens of thousands of years. Each of these kings lived for thousands of years. The obvious conclusion is that all were nonhuman and of extraterrestrial origin. Several of our researchers have spent their lives studying, deciphering these materials. A man named Zachariah Sitchen spent his life deciphering the Sumerian texts. There are now many others, such as Billy Carson, who has researched antiquity for over forty-five years, since 1977. Although I have learned a lot, I always end up confused, due to the level of conjecture and speculation. What is clear is the fact there have been civilizations on this planet for hundreds of thousands of years, probably millions. Secondly, these civilizations have consisted of many races from other worlds. We are missing so much of our history, and the idea that our history only goes back six thousand years is insane. Not long ago, I heard a story of a man in South Carolina, who sent his DNA to one of these lineage services, like Ancestry. com. (It was not Ancestry.com but one very similar.) Anyway, when he received the report, it had traced his linage back over three hundred thousand years. There is so much we do not know, nor understand. A story that really got my attention began in 1935. Two French anthropologists discovered and ancient tribe in western Africa, known as the Dogons. Once they gained the trust of the Dogon shaman, they began hearing of an incredible history. They revealed they had been visited by star people called the Nomos. They talked about the Sirius A and B stars. There was no way they could have known this because only Sirius A could be seen with the naked eye. Sirius B is a white dwarf star. The Dogons said it was the smallest but also the heaviest thing in the cosmos. They named it Potolla, after a tiny seed in West Africa. We now know these white dwarf stars are indeed the densest and heaviest. The question is how could this ancient tribe have known of this. Sirius B is difficult to see today, even with our new telescopes. Furthermore, they spoke of a third star, Sirius C, which we were unable to see until 1995. They also knew of every planet in our solar system and the rotation of each. How could these ancient people have known any of this unless someone from the stars told them? These beings that taught them, were Aquafarians, water beings. This has become a well-known story, one that no one can disprove.

Another story I heard about was the discovery of an iron hammer. It is called the London Hammer. It was dated to around fifty million years ago. Contemporary archeologists and historians do not even want us to talk about this. Many refer to this as "forbidden history." If they cannot explain it, they turn the lights off and refuse to discuss it. This is pure *ego*, another example of a low quality of consciousness. My main reason for injecting these points is to help you to raise your awareness. It sure raised mine.

I have studied a significant amount about ancient civilizations. I do not know what happened back then, because I was not there. However, one thing that has become obvious is that the humans and several extraterrestrials lived and worked, side by side. The Egyptian god Thoth, who was one of the Anunnaki, said he built the Great Pyramid at Giza and oversaw the construction of all the pyramids worldwide. He gave us math and language skills. He also wrote the Emerald Tablets, which have been studied by every important figure in the past several hundred years. He is the one I mentioned earlier that told us of the "dark brothers," the Jedi knights, and the galactic wars between the dark forces and the light. I just ordered a new book called *Compendium of the Emerald Tablets*, by researcher Billy Carson. It is now a bestseller on Amazon and contains a wealth of information and truth.

I recently heard of some discoveries that confirmed that this planet was inhabited by alien races. First, I learned that archeologists have discovered a city under the Great Pyramids at Giza. There are miles of perfectly cut tunnels underneath the entire area. Next, I learned our scientists discovered a city, a civilization, under the ice at Antarctica. They found skeletal remains of humanoid figures over thirty feet tall. I have seen the Nasca Lines in Peru from the air. I have had so many questions about that area for thirty years. I just learned they discovered a city underneath, with miles of tunnels. With the aid of our satellites, there have been huge alien craft, found under the earth, all over the world. No one seems to know how they got there, but they do exist. There is no way any of these underground cities were built by human hands. The proof just keeps adding up. We are missing so much of our history.

# 42

## EVOLUTION OF SECRECY

For decades, the alien presence was the most highly guarded secret in the US government. Grant Cameron found a Canadian document from the Americans, dating back to the 1950s. It stated the following. First, that UFOs are real. Second, that it is the most highly guarded secret in the United States, higher than that of the H-bomb. It also stated there is some psychic or mental phenomenon between humans and the ETs. We now know this was about consciousness. In the early days, following the 1947 Roswell crashes, there were very few people in the loop. They began reverse engineering almost immediately. Now one can only imagine how far they have come in the past seventy-five years. We have had alien reproduction craft in operation for decades. Many of the sightings in recent years were not UAPs, but our own craft.

Most all the true alien craft are cloaked. However, if you get yourself an infrared camera, or telescope, you can see them everywhere. They are visible but not within our normal light spectrum. I saw a couple of documentaries, one called *UFO*, another called *Moon Rising*, both with the subtitle "The Greatest Story Ever Denied." They show thousands of photos and video footage of these craft in the infrared spectrum, both in our atmosphere and in space. They even had a lot taken from our space shuttles.

Earlier, I spoke of the ridicule and harassment of individuals who reported contact with a UFO. This went on for several decades, laughing and making jokes about these people. Well, they are not laughing anymore. The government is no longer denying the existence of aliens, nor their craft. They just are not confirming them. Following the 2017 *New York Times* release of information on the ATIP program, and the subsequent release of gun camera footage of UAPs, many of us have been waking up. I am referring to the 2004 USS *Nimitz* Tic-Tac footage and the 2015 USS *Roosevelt* footage over the Atlantic, called the "Gimble" footage. There is another called "Go Fast." All were later confirmed as authentic by the Department of Defense. The reason this was such a big deal is because it was the first time in our known history that this story was revealed in major news publications and shown on network TV. Prior to this, every story on UFOs, or alien life, had been relegated to the "fringe." In the past, you might have seen a story in a tabloid that might have been true. But because it appeared in a tabloid, most of us discounted it. We have been receiving disclosure since 1947. But it has been drip fed to us. Most everyone agrees the cover-up began with the Roswell crashes. Most of us just did not pay any attention.

It is important to understand this is a worldwide phenomenon, not just an American one. I agree with Paola Harris that the UAP saga has been turned into entertainment in this country. If you go to South America and to Italy, the people accept it as fact and take it seriously. Jaime Mussan, a Mexican investigative journalist, has reported a couple of major stories from Italy. From 1956 to 1978, a group of extraterrestrial beings lived in Milan and had a based under the Adriatic Sea. They lived and interfaced with a wide cross-section of the population, from scientists and politicians to the average person. They came here to help us evolve and live among us. However, in the end they left because of us humans. There is a book, recently translated into English, written by an Italian scientist titled *Mass Contact*. It is an incredible story, with many specific details of what occurred during those years. I am amazed that this story, along with many others, was never picked up by American press. The secrecy has been far worse here than most other countries in the world. In fact, these countries have released their files to their citizens. Only in the United States has there been a truth embargo.

# 43

## DISCLOSURE

Confucius, the ancient Chinese philosopher (501 to 469 BCE) said the following: "True knowledge is to know the extent of one's ignorance." With that being said, I must be getting smarter every day. The more I learn, the less I know.

There are meetings about disclosure taking place daily worldwide. Personally, I do not need politicians to tell me what I already know. Most of them have been bought and paid for by special interest groups, such as the military industrial complex and the Cabal. There is so much evidence available to everyone on this subject. If people would just awaken and begin paying attention, the presence of alien life would be common knowledge to all. I think we will have a government disclosure event, but the question is disclosure of what, and how much. If you only accept the facts presented in this book, you already know much more than they will reveal. In addition, the truth of this phenomenon is already common knowledge to millions of people in this country and worldwide. In my opinion, the only reason they are now giving serious consideration to disclosure is because they can no longer keep a lid on it. I agree with David Adair that "something has happened." He thinks the current push on disclosing is because they feel they are about to get busted for telling the biggest lie in human history for the past seventy-five years.

For years, most of our elected officials were kept in the dark, but this began to change around twenty years ago. I recall a speech given to congress by the late senator from Hawaii Daniel Inouye around 2007. To paraphrase, the senator spoke of a shadow government, with its own air force, navy, its own fund-raising mechanism, free from all checks and balances, and operating above and outside our laws. He hit the nail on the head. This is not only criminal but evil, driven by greed.

I have listened to several panel discussions regarding the subject of disclosure. We know there have been several contracts signed between humans and the ETs. The only thing our people wanted was technology. The question is: What did we give them? We know they wanted human DNA. We also know that thousands of people go missing every year. As was pointed out, how would you like a contract like this to surface with your name on it? Most of the original people behind the secrecy are now dead. New people have taken their place but do not want this secrecy to continue. Several insiders have stated that those in charge today have a higher moral center than those of twenty years ago. This fact does give me hope. The ETs have given us so much technology over the years. Had this technology not fallen into the wrong hands, most of us cannot imagine the world we would be living in today. This has been denied to us by a tiny group of greedy people with more money than they could spend in many lifetimes. It defies the imagination. Here, again, we have another example of a low quality of consciousness. These individuals have not begun to awaken and evolve. They remain hardwired to the physical and material world. What a pity!

A few years ago, the government ceased to use the term UFO. The new term is UAP (unidentified aerial phenomenon). The British came up with it. The reason for the switch is because the term UFO had gathered so much negativity and ridicule over the past decades that many people had closed their minds. Our brains process information like a hard drive. It is stored in compartments. So to open another compartment within our brains, the name was changed to UAP. Frankly, it is a slick way to get people to listen to the truth. There are now committees meeting daily all over the world, to discuss ways to bring about disclosure. It seems that everyone involved has a different agenda. There are those who stand to lose a lot of money, but some of these individuals now understand the necessity of revealing the truth. The age-old question of "Are we alone in the universe?" is long gone. The cat is out of the bag.

One of the biggest concerns about what information to release has to do with: Where did we come from? Although I am a firm believer in telling the truth, the whole truth, and nothing but the truth, I confess I have concern about releasing this truth. Besides, there are differing opinions on this topic. My wife and I have never had secrets, but when I initially heard these truths, I was shaken. Maggie saw this in me and asked what was wrong. I only told her the topic but not the story. To this day, I have never revealed this information to her. She agreed, saying she did not want to know. Everyone has heard the story that we were evolved from an ape species. Even if this is true, it did not occur naturally. Our DNA has been tinkered with. There are countless numbers of researchers who say we came from the stars, that we were seeded here. Whatever the truth, it really does not matter to me. Even if some nonterrestrial beings did tinker with our physical bodies, God made our souls. We are not our bodies.

Another major concern being discussed inside these disclosure groups has to do with the impact on religions. For those who read Scripture with a literal interpretation, it will be a shock. However, for all of us who have studied the major religions, when you get to the core of each, you find the same truths. However, over hundreds of years, they have been filled with so much man-made dogma and become so codified, the truth is elusive. Many of the problems have occurred because churches are built around monetary systems and, yes, even the pursuit of power. The alien species all know of our Creator, of the Golden Rule, and the practice of loving your neighbor as yourself. If you go back to the beginning of the world's greatest religions, you will find it was about being able to confront the divine directly. I completely disagree with those who think our religions will be destroyed. In fact, I am convinced we will need our churches even more. There have been representatives from major religions appearing at meetings on this subject. We know there is something major taking place in Antarctica. We know there is a huge pyramid under the ice, a very old space port, and at least one huge spacecraft. Supposedly, they also discovered a portal there too. No one is allowed access. In 2015, they invited many governmental representatives there. They also invited leaders of various religions. There have been a couple of US presidents who have visited. No one has been able to discover the reasons for this meeting, but it clearly was a "show and tell" of something of great importance. Just recently, four of the scientists working there revealed they had discovered a series of tablets under the ice. He said these tablets told the complete stories of all our religions. He said they did not refute what was in our Bible or any religious scripture. What they did do was to fill in all the gaps of truth and information. I had long felt something was missing from the teachings of Jesus. Then the Nag Hamadi text and the Dead Sea Scrolls were found. They filled in gaps for me and made sense. I suspect the tablets discovered in Antarctica are real and do the same for all religions. However, the powers behind disclosure are terrified to reveal this information to the world. They fear many will reject it and wars could ensue. These same scientists also reported they found sarcophagus of several beings over thirty feet tall. This was deep under the ice. These have also been discovered in other locations around the world.

How will disclosure affect our lives? Every person I have listened to believes disclosure will shift our reality in ways difficult to imagine. It will be a beautiful world. So many people, even the insiders, are sick of all the lies and secrecy. Everyone agrees that lifting the truth embargo is long overdue. One thing most agree on is that it will completely change the medical arena. We live such short lives, especially compared to the ETs, including those who look like us. The technology exists today to heal almost every disease. They can grow or 3D-print any body part or organ. Before his death in 2017, William Thompkins revealed a research program he had been directly involved with. He said there were many major medical companies and institutions involved. Here is what he described: the patient either received four injections or took four pills that look like aspirin. They receive them over a few months. Almost immediately, everything is nicer, and they feel great. Over some time, which he did not specify, the women are reverted to age twenty-one and the men back to age twenty-nine. They remain at that age for a couple of thousand years. I am not sure when he did this interview, but it was not long before his death. He then stated this would be ready and available to a few select people within two years. The only group he mentioned as being a participant in this research was Scripps Hospital in San Diego. I must tell you I have no proof of this but can see no reason he would fabricate a story such as this. I will say that when I consider this possibility with everything I have learned, it does not surprise me. Besides, William Thompkins had a long history of credibility down the street and around the corner. Dr. Robert Wood, who edited Thompkins's last book, said he had long conversations with him on this topic. His credential list is probably even longer than that of Thompkins. I add that regardless of the accuracy of this information, I am positive that our lifetimes will be extended by many years, following disclosure. At my age, it is not about the duration of life, but the quality of my life. To live free of medical problems and disease would be wonderful. It is coming soon.

# 44

## METHODS OF DISCLOSURE

I have learned of many groups meeting to discuss ways to bring about disclosure. The problem is that there does not appear to be a "one group" in charge. Many insiders say the old MJ-12 group, which has changed names many times, is still at the top. What I can tell you is this: I have never seen so much chaos and confusion around one subject. In the United States, you have people from all branches of the military, industrial executives, every three-lettered intelligence group, and now our congressional leaders. Each one has their own agenda. The navy appears to be spearheading the effort. However, this is just within the United States. Then you have groups all over the world, many with differing opinions on how to bring about disclosure. They are discussing two options. The first they refer to as the "take me to your leader plan."

We have ongoing trade and diplomatic relationships with multiple ET races. So the idea is they would have one of them land, like on the White House lawn. The second plan is a false flag invasion. They would contract a species, one that looks nothing like us, and have them do an invasion of Earth. They are talking about an "insectoid" species, which are seven to eight feet tall, which would scare the wits from us. Many humans would die, and we would have worldwide destruction. I know this is hard to believe, or even imagine, but believe me, they are serious. Once the battle begins, we would have other ETs come to our aid and help fight the bad guys. Then, once the battle is over, the good ETs will stick around and help us to rebuild, using all our hidden technology. Again, I am telling you this is being seriously considered.

# 45

## WE HAVE BEEN
## CONTROLLED

We have been almost entirely controlled. In fact, I heard the original plan for disclosure was to be a very slow one, like the slow leaks we have been receiving for decades. However, the tiny handful of individuals controlling of us has gone too far. Michael Jaco, the man I spoke of earlier, who served in the secret space force, on Navy SEAL Team 6, and the CIA, shared a lot of inside information. He said he personally knows of covert teams that have been taking down some of the cabal. Furthermore, Michael spoke of the control exerted on humanity, for thousands of years, by the Draco Reptilians. The Draco are not only our enemies but also enemies to countless other ET species in the cosmos. They have been suppressing our evolution in consciousness throughout our known history. He said they have now been mostly removed from Earth and from this part of our galaxy. There are still a few pockets of them, and they are hard to locate. They can shape-shift their appearance to look just like humans. One way to spot them is that when you look them in the eye, and they get a little angry, you see a slit eye. There are many stories floating around that say the "blue bloods" and the royal families are Reptilian.

William Thompkins shared a story in an interview about being approached by a woman in a meeting. She and her husband, along with three other couples, had a party one Friday night. The following morning, one couple wanted to show the others where their new condo was being built. So they went out and were standing on this hillside, which was on the border of Oceanside and Carlsbad, California. They were taking pictures, looking out, not upward, just across this little valley. They saw nothing, but when they got the pictures developed, they were shocked at what appeared in the photos. According to Bill Thompkins, there were six Reptilian tankers, dispersing four different gases out the back. He said these gases were mind-controlling agents. He had given a copy to Dr. Robert Wood, who had the photos examined, and they were deemed authentic. I saw the pictures, and the craft were crystal clear, as were the gases being dispersed. In recent years, I have heard stories of "chemtrails," coming from airliners. Some alien species, like the Draco, can use holographic projections to make one of their craft appear as an airliner and spray gases into our atmosphere. He continued by describing situations where groups have been briefed on the UAP phenomenon, nod their heads in agreement, then completely forget everything thirty minutes later. He shared other accounts that were very similar. This made no sense to me. Why would anyone want to keep humanity in ignorance and asleep? Still, Bill Thompkins, before his death, swore this was happening. Although he spent over seven decades working in the above-top-secret world, no one knows where he got this information from. Even he admitted it was a fantastic story but stated this has indeed been happening.

This next story is one that has haunted me since I first hear it a few months ago.

A government insider, whom I completely trust, said there was an "above-top-secret" meeting three years ago. It was held at a secret location. Attending were members of all the intelligence agencies. He does not know what they were told, but when they came out of the meeting, they were stunned, white as sheets. The only thing he was able to learn was they were told that something is going to happen between now and 2027. Again, there is the year of 2027, which I have heard so many times. Regardless of what our people decide regarding disclosure, there exists another variable they cannot control. I am referring to the ETs.

Perhaps they told them something is coming. We do know they have been present at many disclosure meetings. What concerns me is they may have been told of a catastrophic event approaching. The ultimate shift! I pray I am wrong. If this is the case, they would not tell us. Of all the thousands of pieces of information I have gathered, this story went right though my heart. Perhaps because the truth has a ring to it, and resonated within me.

# 46

## WHOM DO WE TRUST
## FOR TRUTH?

The individuals I find myself trusting are those who have had direct contact with ETs. First, there are the abduction cases. Next, there are people like Emery Smith, who worked alongside various ETs races in the secret special-access projects. Over the past year, I have viewed many interviews of a German man known only as Tim. He is a technical adviser to the covert government in Germany on ET agendas on earth. He says he has had well over a hundred meetings, face to face, with extraterrestrials. There are a couple of things which all these people agree on. First, not one of these people sense the ETs pose a threat to us. Second, they all say the ETs have told them that humans have a greater potential for becoming highly evolved than any species in the universe. If we can just get past this fighting among each other, we can become a major player in the cosmos. Now back to the question of why someone would wish to keep us asleep. The Draco have been here for thousands of years. They know our potential and fear us for that reason. They want to keep us under tight control. We now know the Nazis worked with them. It is widely accepted that select human groups are connected to them. Here again, I am referring to the Cabal. I have no proof of this, but one thing for certain is that the motives of both are identical. I am aware this is difficult to imagine, but there is a mountain of evidence to validate this as truth. It is critical for us to keep an open mind when looking at this topic.

I remember growing up, being taught that the earth is the center of the universe. We know we are part of the Milky Way galaxy. We also now know there are at least two hundred trillion galaxies. I was surprised to learn that Earth is out on the far rim of the milky way. We are out in the boonies and far from "downtown" in our galaxy. This is part of the reason we have remained unaware of other civilizations existing in the Milky Way. Another thing we have learned from the aliens is how interesting our planet is to them. For them, coming here is like going to Disneyland. Virtually every alien civilization has just one race. Only on Earth do we have multiple races of people. Equally amazing is that we have millions of life forms. Other planets only have a few, but here there are millions, in the air, the oceans, under the surface, and on the land. There are planets in the cosmos, with human civilizations, that began close to the same time as us. However, they are much more advanced than we are. The reason is because they had only one race, but mostly because they have not been controlled by an intensely greedy group of people. The ETs are waiting on us to grow up and evolve into the fourth density. This is when we realize we are not different from our neighbor, regardless of human race or any other species of sentient being. We are all of one consciousness. When this occurs, we then learn the meaning of what Jesus taught: love thy neighbor as thyself. What we do here on Earth has a direct impact on the evolution of consciousness in the universe. Somehow, our evolution has a direct impact on them. This is why the ETs are here, trying to help us. They all want us to succeed.

As for the disclosure projects, there is indeed much confusion and lack of agreement. Still, they all know we are rapidly running out of time. This must happen, and soon. The "shift" is happening now. We have no choice in whether it occurs or not. First, the earth itself is shifting. Our poles are moving. Secondly, everything in our galaxy is moving. I confess, some of this is beyond my pay grade, but I will dumb it down, as it was dumbed down for me. As earth moves into alignment with the galactic equator, we are now receiving galactic rays, coming from the galactic black hole. These rays, all energy, are now upgrading our frequency to the fourth harmonic density. This is why millions of people are awakening now. I am not a big news observer, but am told the topic of consciousness is appearing everywhere. This has never occurred in our known history. The "shift" is happening right now. If we fail to evolve, it could mean the end of us, or we are pushed back to the Stone Age. As humans, we love to argue. Everyone has an opinion, and some feel that anyone who does not agree with them is wrong. Having said this, the shift I am referring to is not open for debate. It would be like arguing about whether water is wet. However, we all have free choice. You can choose to keep your head buried in the sand, or you can choose to awaken and accept truth.

Even though those members of the disclosure projects know the shift is happening, still there remain a few who want to keep things as they are. I spoke of the Draco Reptilians controlling us for thousands of years. They have not done this alone. Whether humans consciously joined with them or not, the fact is they are a huge part of the problem. Again, I point out that we have been almost completely controlled by what is called a "feudal system." Here, we have most of the wealth in the hands of a few people, and the rest of us are treated like cattle. We must move to a type-one civilization, or we all perish. In a type one, everyone is a citizen, the wealth is spread out, no poverty, almost no crime, and no hunger. The list goes on and on. It is not surprising that those with the money want to keep things as they are, but not all of them. They are beginning to realize that if we do not become a transparent society and evolve, there will be nothing left for anyone. They can keep their wealth, but no human needs trillions of dollars.

Overall, disclosure is a very fluid discussion. They all seem to agree it must happen, but how this will occur is the question. My prayer is they do not move forward with the false flag invasion. I am convinced the more people who become aware of this plan, the less likely they are to go in that direction. In my opinion, this idea is insane. Not long ago, I was watching a panel discussion on disclosure. David Adair was one of the participants. They asked each one how would they handle disclosure. David Adair said he would just tell it all and let the chips fall where they may. They all laughed, and Tim said, "Wow, now that is radical." Frankly, I tend to agree with David. This is because I am a true believer that truth will set you free. David pointed out that this mess all started back in the 1940s, when they began with the lies. Now, over seventy-five years later, they have added so many layers of lies, involving so many different agencies and people, it is like a giant open wound. The wound must be healed, or else. So you take a hot poker and stick it to the wound to stop the bleeding and heal it. As David said, "It is going to hurt like hell," but it must be done. Then we can move on. I agree it is a complicated issue, and I understand why so many are concerned about how people will react, not to mention the disruption it may cause to society. Yet no one person, no nation, no planet, can have a healthy life based on lies. I probably know more about this subject than 90 percent of the world population, and yes, the truth will be painful for many of us. I have witnessed many times, on a personal basis, how someone has suppressed the truth over years. This has created so much pain and dysfunction. Still, in an instant, a psychologist can bring the truth out into the open, shine light on it, and the person is transformed instantly. It is a beautiful thing to witness. I had my own experience with the same thing, which I described in my book *Shining Bear.*

They seem to want seventy-five years of lies, an open wound, to be healed without pain and no disruption. This simply cannot happen, regardless of how they do it. I would much prefer to get the pain over with in one treatment. If we know anything about humanity, it is that we can adapt to most anything. Some people are going to be very angry to learn how they have been lied to. I have often thought of where we would be today had they told us the truth, after the Corona crash in 1947. All the technology would be in the public domain. We would be traveling to the stars, exploring, just like on *Star Trek.* I am far from being the only person who has contemplated this. All agree we would be traveling the cosmos; our lives would be extended by at least a hundred years.

I have talked about the "think tanks" on disclosure. There are similar meetings taking place worldwide every week. What I have not shared is the fact there are ETs participating in several of these groups. Do you remember in *Star Trek*, they always spoke of the Federation of Planets? It turns out this is true. Paul Hellyer, the late former Canadian defense minister and longtime member of Parliament, often spoke of this federation. In 2020, the Israeli space security chief, Haim Eshed, spoke of the Federation of Planets. Mr. Eshed said that when the encounter took place, then President Trump knew about it, and so did several other world leaders. At the time it was decided that humanity was not ready for this revelation. It turns out, there are many federations in the cosmos.

# 47

## UNITED FEDERATION
## OF HENDON

Last year, I learned about the one called "the United Federation of Hendon." It consists of 574 planets, and most look like us. This information came from a man named Jerimiah Davis, who spent thirty years in the CIA. He was then drafted into the federation as an ambassador. He was given the title of a four-star general and traveled with them throughout the galaxy. He passed away a few years ago, and a woman took his place, meaning we are still represented. The man who shared this story is Duane Ollinger, a Texas oil driller who owns 160 acres of land in Utah, now called the Blind Frog Ranch. This story is like the one of Skinwalker Ranch, located close by. He saw their spacecraft, nine of them, on his ranch. It is an incredible story, too long to go into here. Duane was directed to do some drilling on his property. They unearthed some very strange phenomena. Davis and the federation were overseeing all of this, over a few years. He went to visit Jermiah Davis on his deathbed and was asked to reveal this story to the world. He could not decline because he felt he owed a favor. His daughter was on her deathbed several years earlier in Amarillo, Texas. Her case was hopeless. He explained that as a normal person's triglycerides are around 300, and someone with a count of 800 is deadly; his daughter had a level of 13,000. They saved her life. He said they parked a spacecraft over the hospital and bombarded it with healing frequencies. They also put boots on the ground and worked on her directly. Duane is not an educated man, but he is an intelligent person. I could not help but believe him. He is so genuine. He shared many stories told to him by Davis, such as the fact that he and the federation had meetings with Putin, Trump, leaders in India, and others. One story, which I had seen in the news, was of a craft over the "Dome of the Rock" in Jerusalem. The alien craft shot a beam down into the dome. Duane said Jeramiah Davis told him, "That was us." What we were not told was that someone had placed a "baby nuclear device" inside. The beam shut it down, and then the Israeli defense forces went in and cleaned it up. He shared other stories like one with North Korea, where they were getting out of control and how the issue was resolved. They went to President Trump and provided an advanced technology, which was used to threaten North Korea. I remember Trump taking credit for getting them to back off.

The reason I shared the federation story with you is that it is important to know we are being helped. They are watching over us. This is comforting for me to know. They want us to become a part of this federation, but first, we must stop our warring ways. This has been the consistent message from all the extraterrestrials. Another consistent message is that humans are charged with being stewards of this planet and that we are doing a terrible job. I could not agree more, but what is worse is that we have the technology to clean it up in a few days. Yet someone does not want this to happen. I cannot understand a human motive that would object to cleaning our home. The explanation is that it would mean they must reveal the technology, from all the back engineering. This is like saying a man is dying from a horrific disease. He has the cure but does not use it because someone might find out he has it. Insanity?

Every piece of information I have written here is available in the public domain. I acknowledge there is a lot of misinformation out there, counterintelligence and just outright lies. I listen mostly to private researchers, like Lina Moulton Howe, Paoli Harris, and many others who have now passed. I am referring to people like the late astronaut Dr. Edgar Mitchell, Dr.

J. Allen Hynick, Dr. Stan Freedman, Dr. Jacque Valle, and many others. I strongly recommend that if you want the truth, turn off network TV and start watching Gaia TV. I cannot begin to tell you how much I have learned by watching various shows on Gaia, like *Cosmic Disclosure, Beyond Belief with George Noury,* and many others. There are many series on Gaia that get into all aspects of human existence. I doubt we will ever get the truth from mainstream media, nor from our government. They seem to think we are stupid, too weak to handle the truth. In my opinion, they fear loss of control over the world population. However, due to the shift taking place, they are backed into a corner. They know the truth must come out, but they want to spoon-feed it to us in bits and pieces. It is clear to many of us that something has happened. Prior to 2017, no one in government, nor mainstream media would mention this topic. Now it is in the news constantly. Suddenly, they appear to be pushing disclosure forward. They are leaking one piece of information after another. We are being climatized, "broken in," on the UAP presence. I would love to know what happened. Was it human or alien? Whatever occurred, something did and they are reacting. Some researchers refer to it as a "knee-jerk" reaction, and they fear being caught in the biggest lie in human history.

# 48

## HOW HUMANS CAN SOLVE
## HUMAN PROBLEMS

Earlier in this book, I spoke of how humans must reach a critical mass to evolve in consciousness. In 1960, a yogi from India proposed that we could improve the quality of life with only 1 percent of the population. In 1974, he gathered a group of people to meditate in a city with high crime. They sent out love energy. Suddenly the crime rate dropped like a rock. When they ceased, the crime rate went back up. This became known as the "Maharishi effect," after the yogi, Maharishi Mahesh. In the early 2000s, a group doing meditations was organized in Washington, DC. Crime was out of control. During the period this was taking place, crime dropped over 23 percent. David Wilcock talked of a study where seven thousand meditators sent out love energy to the world. Suddenly terrorism and violence dropped 72 percent. From a scientific method perspective, the results have been reproduced consistently on a worldwide basis. It also provides additional proof that all consciousness is connected. We can change the world if we come together. First, we must get past this delusion of being helpless, just our physical bodies, and limited. We are connected to everything in the universe. The same energy that flows through everything out there flows through each of us. We are just light, energy, consciousness, and connected to everything, including God. We can effect change at the speed of thought. If we can only awaken to this fact, we can solve our problems. In addition, by awakening, we remove the control that has been placed over us by the Cabal. They do know this and have done everything possible to keep these truths secret. Please believe me, they want us to remain asleep. This is not just about the reverse engineering, all the technology held in secret, but the truth about who we are and the power each of us has. Many have suggested they have a sickness; they feed on the power and control they have over us. Otherwise, there is no logic to their actions. Only we can remove their control by awakening to the truth.

If you think this "shift" I have been referring to is fiction, a fairy tale, I suggest you investigate quickly. Every researcher, scientist, quantum physicist, theologian, and even government official knows this is not only real, but also happening now. We know there are countless numbers of ET spacecraft, of countless races, orbiting this planet. They have told us this is coming and are watching Earth to witness what occurs. They are not allowed to interfere. This is what makes me think the shift is imminent. Why would they be out there watching now if this was to occur years from now? No one on Earth knows when this event will happen but I suspect the aliens do, or at least have a good idea. The spoken word is powerful. The German adviser Tim started a movement for everyone to say this mantra: "All shift happily now." I say this every day, at least once. We can help ourselves to make the shift a good and happy one. I can tell you this: you have more power than you ever dreamed possible, just by going within and using your soul, spirit, or consciousness. These terms all reflect the same meaning.

In our culture, we revere intellect. We put scientists and academics on pedestals because of their intellect. I am certainly guilty of doing this. Furthermore, I still do and am certainly not trying to minimize high intellect in any way. However, I have learned a question must be asked. Do they have the wisdom of the soul, of Christ consciousness? As one researcher stated, "If they do not, they are like the village idiots insofar as true knowledge." I will attempt to explain; for decades, I have said things like "If you want to be close to God, you must be out of your mind." In my prayer and meditation, I sometimes have trouble shutting my brain off.

When we enter the spirit world of universal consciousness, we can access all knowledge in the cosmos, from the beginning of time to now. One of the most brilliant people ever was Nicola Tesla. He told people he was getting information and ideas from outside himself, maybe from ETs. A hundred years ago, no one paid any attention, but they sure are now. By going within, we can have direct communication with Jesus, and with many other conscious beings in the universe.

We have heard the term Galactic Federation for years. It is comprised of many races of sentient beings who are highly evolved. They want to help us to evolve, awaken, and ascend. However, they are not allowed to interfere with the natural order of evolution. This includes any species. However, if we learn to make conscious contact with them, they will answer any question we have and provide us with almost infinite knowledge. There are now thousands of people worldwide who are doing this.

There are many species who belong to this Galactic Federation, which is an alliance of planets. Before I begin describing them, it is critical that I first explain these are large star systems. They contain a variety of species within each. Here, I am only referring to the ones we know about that belong to this federation. We know of five key species. There are the Arthurian, which are 4.5 to 5.5 feet tall, with light-blue skin, large heads, and almond-shaped eyes. Next are the Andromedins, which are six to ten feet tall, with light-blue skin and very slender builds. A third species are the Pleiadeans. They look like us and are here on Earth now, working with the government and assisting to reverse engineer technology. They come from a star group we refer to as the Seven Sisters. Then we have those from Sirius. Some of them are Aquafarians, water people, and the ones who taught the Dogon tribe in West Africa. All these beings are highly evolved spiritual beings. The fifth species are the Felines. They are said to be the oldest race in our galaxy. Yes, they resemble cats but are humanoid. They are here now and have been trying to help us for thousands of years. If you go to India and look at their ancient artwork, you will see blue beings everywhere. I have heard many researchers question who these blue beings were. Now we know. Recently, I have watched several interviews of highly credible and conscious people who have experienced direct contact with some of these beings. One woman has been interfacing with an Arthurian since childhood. She has a name for him, eHee, and describes him as her teacher. She said Hee, and all members of his species, are here to help us take the next leap in consciousness. This is not speculation! There is so much data to support this is happening; it simply cannot be denied. The members of the federation are here to help us, but they cannot do it for us. We must grow up and awaken on our own. They are standing by to help, and all we need to do is ask. How do we ask? We must practice meditation and learn to communicate directly with them. I need to point out that these beings are vibrating at a much higher frequency than humans. This means they cannot appear in our 3D, in their true appearance. They often appear as light, or plasma beings, with large auras around them. This may explain why, in ancient times, they were often mistaken for angels. The late Edgar Casey also said the Arthurians were the most spiritually advanced civilization. They can do much for us, insofar as helping us to evolve in consciousness and assisting us in ascension. The Andromedins are master builders of space craft. We know they are a nomadic species. They live on giant biospheres the size of large cities. Many insiders believe they built our moon. Regardless, they have certainly assisted humans in constructing our space vehicles. If you look at the logo of every space agency on earth, you will see an *A* symbol. I do not know if this is connected, but it is interesting to contemplate. This is true even with the Chinese space agency, even though they use characters versus letters. Yet they use this symbol.

The five races I mentioned are not the only species we know of. For example, there are multiple races of Reptilians, Insectoids, ant people, Gray aliens, and the list seems endless. The late Clifford Stone spoke of fifty-seven species known by our government. Of all the people I have listened to on this topic, I have never questioned anything Stone said, nor do I know of anyone who has. A sweeter soul was never born. His death was a great loss. He worked as an "Interfacer" with various alien species for years while he was in the military.

In the first part of this book, I spoke of the teachings of the Gnostics and the Ascenes. The Ascenes were said to have been living with, and being taught by, angels and extraterrestrials. Perhaps these ETs were of one of the species I mentioned above. However, they also spoke of a group of aliens they called the Arkonians, the Arkon. They were evil and trying to take over the minds of humans. The Apostle Paul wrote about them, warning us. They sound exactly like the Draco Reptilians, which we talk about today. They feed on fear, a dark energy. Paul and the Gnostics spoke of how they invaded the minds of leaders, whether kings or politicians. They encourage *ego* in these individuals, which invariably leads to greed and hunger for power. Today, we refer to the 1 percenters, the Cabal. The Ascenes, the Gnostics, and the Apostle Paul recommended us to stay away from these afflicted leaders. They knew two thousand years ago that fear was the enemy of the human soul. Today, we appear to finally be catching up. This knowledge increased dramatically when science and religion joined together. Nicola Tesla said that the day science began to study the unseen, we would gain more ground in ten years than in the previous centuries combined. That day has arrived. I have observed that low-conscious humans thrive on fear, which manifests in several negative ways, especially anger. I stay as far away from these individuals as possible. The exception is only if they ask for help. This goes back to the age-old battle between good and evil. The most important thing I can point out is very simple; each of us has a choice. We have free will and can choose to live in fear or in love. The native American Indians say this: We each have two wolves inside us. One is loving and compassionate. The other is mean and violent. Then they pose the question: Which one will win today? The answer is the one you feed the most. It is a daily choice we all must make.

Earlier I spoke of a story by William Thompkins and Dr. Robert Wood. I am referring to the photo taken of Draco Reptilian space tankers spraying gases over Southern California. I mention this again because I recently learned that in 2003, a group of scientists discovered a molecule in the human brain. It was out of place, and there was no reason it should be there. They call it, PP-1, protein phosphatase one. What is its effect? It suppresses memory. Clearly someone placed it there. In the first part of this book, I stated that we have been called a species with amnesia. We have forgotten who we truly are.

Today, I often think of people on other planets, in other star systems. My perception has shifted, and my level of awareness has expanded exponentially. Through this, my consciousness has certainly evolved. I never feel alone anymore. I know I am connected to not only God, and Jesus, but also to every sentient being in the cosmos. Today, I feel love and compassion for all. I invite each of you to join me on this exciting journey. The truth will absolutely set you free. I know this for a fact because it has done so for me, and I am just like you.

# 49

## TAKING HUMAN
## INVENTORY

When I began my research and investigation on the UAP phenomenon, I went down the rabbit hole. I knew there had been a great deal of secrecy surrounding this subject, but I had no idea just how deep the lies went. Yes, I have learned a lot of details, a few of which I have shared here. The most shocking revelation has been my discovery of how we have been controlled. The controls were installed so gradually, we never noticed. Humans have the capability to adapt quickly. Suddenly, even terrible living conditions become normal. Consider how many wars we have fought since WWII. This did not happen by accident. These wars were orchestrated by the military industrial complex and the Cabal, which are often the same thing. We spend our lives focused outside our-selves. We worry about keeping a roof over our heads and food on the table. By the time we get home from work, we are too tired to think about the subject mat-ter contained here. Every one of us has been engaged in this manner of living. I am not suggesting we cease doing these things. I am only recommending we take a few minutes every day to meditate and pray. Take time to think of these things when alone in your car, discussing it with your spouse and your friends. The most critical thing is to look within your own heart. Failure to do this results in living a life of fear. Many years ago, when I stepped onto my spiritual path, I did not believe myself to be a fearful person. When I be-gan examining my behavior, looking at my anger, judg-ment of others, and my reactions to various things, I was stunned. Fear manifests within us in so many ways. In my case, I realized it had come about so gradually, I considered it normal. However, once I recognized it, I began to eliminate it, one fragment at a time. As I got rid of many of my fears, love entered my life, and my consciousness began to rise.

The control over humanity is nothing new. I can-not offer a date, but it certainly goes back to biblical times. Back then, the people were controlled by kings and queens and dictators. Then the church gained control. Today in this country, we take for granted the freedoms we have. This country was built by people arriving here to escape oppression, from religious to land ownership. Now we are being controlled again, in different ways.

This is the biggest story in the history of humanity. The reality we have known all our lives, from written human history, is changing. We are at the precipice of a new world and a new reality, one that will take us among the stars. This is not just a story. It is not a fictional sci-fi movie; it is real. I just had a birthday and am now seventy-four. I do not know how many years of life I have remaining, but I strongly believe it may come in my lifetime. I continue to hear 2027 and have heard this several times. I do not know if it will begin that year or whether it is the year of the complete shift. No one knows the answer, but I do know it could occur at any moment. We must strive to be ready in our heart, our soul, and our mind. This has become the most important goal in my life. We must awaken to who we really are, leave our ego at the door, and walk away from the self-centeredness and materialism. Leave behind the thoughts of being unworthy, limited, and realize we are so much more, that we are spiritual beings having a physical experience. In my book *Shining Bear*, I spoke of the fact there are only two core emotions: love and fear. I first learned this over thirty years ago but at the time did not have a full understanding of the overall meaning. Perhaps I still do not, but I have come a long way. I now know the most important thing we must remove from our lives is *fear*. Fear is the enemy of the soul. I am not speaking of good fears but fear of death, fear of everything we do not understand or know about, such as the presence of alien life in the cosmos. We must practice living our lives with "an attitude of gratitude." No one can feel grateful and be in fear simultaneously. Jesus spoke of worry, asking if it has ever added anything good to our lives. Fear distorts everything. In fear, we invariably make poor choices and take inappropriate actions. Instead of loving our neighbors as ourselves, we fear them, especially if they appear different from us.

Back in the 1940s, when our military first encountered alien craft and alien beings, many were terrified. This fear extended to the president, the generals, and the scientists involved. I am not judging these people. I might have reacted the same way. The problem was they reacted out of fear, and their decisions on deceiving the public were all based on fear. Then greed took over with many of them. Instead of trying to understand the alien races, all they could see was the technology, which translated to dollar signs. I suspect they never intended things to get this far, but once we tell a lie, at least ten more lies appear to cover that lie. Now here we are, some seventy-five years later, with a huge mess.

The real problem is that most all the original people in the loop, whether military, intelligence officers, or scientists, reacted out of fear. I mean no disrespect to them. but it is so unfortunate that these were the groups who had direct contact. Most of the scientists, although brilliant people, still believed everything is just matter, of a physical and material universe. The military and the intelligence people see everything as a threat. Their job is to serve and protect. They completely missed the most important issues, which have to do with evolution of consciousness and spirituality. They saw technology that was hundreds and thousands of years more advanced than what we had. Yes, it is true the technology was far advanced and is understandable that they wanted to learn about it, and reverse engineer it. However, their reaction was like meeting a person with a great automobile and only seeing the owner as someone with a great car. They never really thought about the owner. Anyone can see the level of ignorance in that kind of thinking, but this is what occurs when operating from fear. It is not difficult to understand that a species that could be a million years older than us would be more technologically advanced. However, it appears they never considered they might also be far more advanced in consciousness, and spiritually, than us. Perhaps the worst thing was their assumption that the aliens thought as they did. They must be here to conquer us, to kill us. Nothing could have been further from the truth. Besides, we had nothing they wanted or needed.

# 50

## ETS APPEARING ON EARTH

We are not seeing as many UAPs today as in the past. The reason is our people are shooting them down. They want to get access to the technology. Many of the sightings now are ARVs, alien reproduction vehicles. They are coming and going all the time but are cloaked. If you want to see them, get yourself a camera or a scope with an infrared lens, and I am told they appear constantly. We just cannot see them with the naked eye.

I told you there are countless numbers of alien craft outside our atmosphere. I know this is true because I saw video of them. Several years ago, one of our space shuttles was orbiting the earth. They had launched a satellite with a twelve-mile tether attached. The tether broke and was traveling with the shuttle. On board were both infrared and UV cameras. In the NASA video, Houston called up, asking the astronauts what they were seeing. They were only seeing the tether, but on the ground, the video feed was showing huge spacecraft everywhere. By using the twelve-mile-long tether, which glowed white, they could accurately judge the size of these craft. They varied in size, but some were longer than the tether. I still do not know how this video leaked out, but it did. We know they are indeed out there.

I recently watched an interview with Paoli Harris, who has traveled the world as a UFO field investigator. I was already aware that this subject is treated very differently in other countries. She spoke of South America and how the people take this seriously. I knew this was true in Peru, as I had spent a lot of time there. She said they had numerous cases of UAPs landing and aliens getting out, with many people present, including journalists. This is happening in Chile, Colombia, Brazil, and other countries there. They know, and have known for decades, the truth of alien life. They accept it with little question. Most other countries have already released their UFO files. Only in the United States are they still hanging onto the theory that its citizens not ready for the truth, cannot handle the truth. The only answer as to the continued secrecy is "special interest groups."

I never realized how much we have been controlled by a small group of wealthy individuals on a global basis. We have wars being fought over nothing. Both sides are being controlled in these conflicts, by this same group. They have us in the middle, like puppets. We end up fighting and killing each other when we should be fighting them. How many eighteen-year-old boys have died, just so these people could make money?

Over the last hundred years, there have been many inventors who have developed game-changing technology. For example, a man named Stanley Meyer in Ohio developed a car that would run on water. He was harassed and finally murdered. Others have developed power sources, such as zero-point energy devices, and were either killed or shut down fast. Think about it: technology out there that could cut your electrical bills by 80 percent overnight. Technology that can run our cars without every buying gasoline again. We do not have this because it impacts the pocketbooks of the few. Worse yet, it is destroying our atmosphere. I wonder how much illness is created due to the dirty air we breathe and the water we drink.

The only way we can change our situation, get out from under the thumbs of this small group, is to awaken. Once we all become aware of the truth, we can regain control over our lives and take away the power of the few. We have all been guilty of sleepwalking through life. I know I was for many years. We get caught up into our routines, are busy trying to feed our families and keep a roof over our heads. We turn on the news, which is *controlled by this same group.* Without realizing it, we are being brainwashed, only told what they want us to believe. This is why many of us have ceased watching the news. In this country, just look at the political situation. I see so many people enraged at the opposing leader or party. They are pitting one side against the other. Again, our problem has little to do with politics. It is all about a "low quality of consciousness." The ETs must be frustrated with us. The next time you hear the word "threat" associated with UAPs, remember that almost all of this is being orchestrated by the same small group. To be clear, I am not suggesting that evil does not exist in the universe. Of course, it does, but even those military people in the know say that 95 percent of the ET races are benevolent. Still, we continue to hear the word "threat," again and again. I agree with Emery Smith when he said if you want to see a hostile species, go look in the mirror. We murder each other. Today, it is crystal clear they have been coming to this planet for thousands of years. If they wanted to harm us, they could have wiped us out at any time with the push of a button. Instead, they have been helping us all along, and still are today.

We have ET life among us, under our feet, and everywhere. It is not a question of why they are not exposing themselves. They have been, but we had to learn where to look. They are hiding in plain sight.

# 51

## CONCLUSIONS

Many years ago, when I first became interested in this subject, I just wanted to know whether we are alone in the universe. Today, I have learned there are thousands of sentient life forms, just within our galaxy. In addition, they are walking among us, both on the surface and in the honeycomb pockets under the surface. I have learned so many things I had never dreamed possible. I learned we have missions taking place daily, through portals, that instantly take the teams to other planets. They also have teams going through similar portals deep into the earth, where they have discovered countless life forms of sentient life and plants that do not exist on the surface. We are now seeing new medicines and technology from reverse engineering the samples these groups have returned with.

Earlier, I told you the ETs all have some human DNA. In turn, we all have some alien DNA. One day soon, we will be able to send our DNA to a service and learn which alien species our ancestry originates from. The database already exists. There are said to be twelve alien races we are genetically linked to. I suspect mine is from the Pleiadean star system. Although there are different species there, most look like us and are tall, with blue eyes and blond hair. I am a fit physically, having had blond hair as a kid.

I have learned of technology that is so far advanced, I have not told you about it. If I did, many of you would not believe me. This is especially true with medical devices. Most remains hidden, but look around at all the new advances we have seen. Almost all comes from reverse-engineered ET technology. I do not want to show disrespect for the scientists who have been involved because without them, these advances would not be possible. Virtually all advances in our electronics over the last seventy years came from them.

I have spoken of the need for us to awaken and evolve in consciousness. This is critical for each of us spiritually but also important as we advance in technology. Most all the alien craft are flown by conscious-assisted technology. In fact, many of the craft are "alive," conscious themselves. They have taken samples from them and discovered they contained the same DNA as the being operating and flying them. We have tried to copy this. I have learned we now have built neuro-link technology to fly our spacecraft with no manual controls being necessary.

I had a friend ask, "How did we learn of these honeycomb pockets in inner earth?" As I understand it, they began when new satellites were developed with ground penetrating radar, where they can do a kind of x-ray through the earth. Next, a scientist developed a "low ground-penetrating radar" device that can see through the earth. It can provide details of everything there. The scientists have now built a holographic inner-earth map. This system has revealed many things from large pockets of white gold, to many spacecrafts buried there.

The extraterrestrials have certainly been helping us. Researchers now agree they have left craft for us to find. These craft appeared with no occupants. They had not crashed and were in perfect working order. They have entered craft with certain frequences. Emery Smith said he had a blood-borne disease, and one of the scientists had cancer, tumors. They both experienced spontaneous healings and later determined it was from the frequency. This was back-engineered and may be available to the public soon. I could literally write another book just on the technologies I have learned about.

The ETs know everything we have built in these underground special-access projects. They have made it clear they are not happy that these technologies have been held in secrecy. Linda Moulton Howe has worked with at least two individuals who had received downloads of binary code into their minds. They had contacted Linda, and she had the code deciphered by experts. The messages were warnings of upcoming events. They stated that all hidden technology must be revealed to all citizens if we were to survive. It is upsetting to know of life-changing technology that can save lives and eliminate human suffering worldwide. Greed is the only reason we do not have access to these incredible advances. The way this is explained is simple; I heard there is already an iPhone 25 that will have an application that can scan anywhere on your body, four hundred times better than a CAT scan, and spot cancer cells. Then you press another button that will zap the cancer and destroy it instantly. Now we ask why do they not make this available today. The reason is because they want to make money from iPhone 15, 16, 20, 22, and so forth. Although I am told this technology does now exist, I am just using this as an example. The same holds true in every area of technology. They could reduce our energy cost today to almost zero, but first they want to introduce a technology that may reduce if by 10 percent, then 20 percent, and so on.

For years, I had heard about an antigravity electromagnetic propulsion flying device called the TR3-B. Members of the secret space force reported being flown to the moon in on it. The flight was less than an hour. I had no way of knowing whether this existed, but neither could I discount it. Then only recently, someone dumped the patent for it on the internet. It has been in operation for at least thirty years. They simply cannot keep the lid on this anymore. The truth is coming out one way or another. Just as Ben Rich said in 1993, we now have the technology to take ET home. Although I had never doubted his words, I now know he was being truthful. We have been traveling to the stars for many years. This has been limited to a select few members of the Cabal and members of the secret space force. Frankly, I am surprised the Galactic Federation has allowed this. I do know that before the mass of humanity will be allowed to travel into the galaxy, we must first evolve in consciousness. We must awaken to who we truly are, all of one consciousness, netted with all sentient life in the universe and multiverse. We must evolve out of this fear-based 3D reality and into the fourth and fifth harmonic frequency, a love-based frequency. We have proven ourselves to be a "warring species," and this must cease. This is what the federation has been waiting for. The shit is imminent and happening now.

Approximately fifteen years ago, an international group of scientists discovered that we are approaching a major shift on this planet. I was told that this information was originally revealed to them by the ETs. The earth has gone through several shifts, about every fifteen thousand years. The last one was what we refer to as the great flood. Naturally, this was a shocking revelation. Initially, they kept this news quiet. They had to investigate and confirm. They wasted no time and have verified this as a fact. We are already seeing increased solar activity, and the poles are shifting. We receive our energy from the sun. As the solar activity increases, we humans are now receiving higher energy and radiation. This is why so many people are awakening, all over the world. The ETs have told us this shift is going to be a good thing. They are helping us in many ways I do not understand, even with the pole shift. I do find myself comforted by this. I know that we have no technology that can accomplish these things. While I cannot confirm this firsthand, I can say I have heard this from multiple sources, both Americans and Europeans.

In conclusion, we are capable of such deep love, compassion, and selflessness. In addition, we are a highly creative race of beings and possess so much potential. I know there will be some readers who may reject much of this information. Emery Smith, who spent years working in the secret-access projects, said trust no one about this phenomenon. I tell you the same thing. Do not take my word for any of this; find out for yourself. The information is available to every one of you. I can tell you that I am a man of truth. I would never knowingly lie to you. I care too much about my own soul to lie. I know it is poison for my soul. Some of you, who have not been informed on this topic, will think I have given you such a wealth of information. For the insiders, it would be considered elementary.

Perhaps the most frustrating part of writing this book is the fact I was unable to include so many things. There are areas I have not even touched on and many I have barely scratched the surface with. Everything I have discussed here has come from highly credible sources. I have also cross-referenced all the key points, hearing the same facts from multiple individuals, with no apparent relationship to one another. I am not a scientist, a researcher, nor a ufologist. I am an "observer." As in quantum mechanics, we know that an observer changes the probabilities in everything. I ask each of you to become observers. If I could ask one thing from each of you, it would be to please, please, wake up. We have all overslept. Every insider knows this is the most important story in human history. You may have previously thought the UAP story was a joke. We have been conditioned to think this way over many decades. It came about in a methodical and systematic way, meaning we have been suckered by counterintelligence operatives into thinking this way.

Perhaps you have simply had no interest, thinking, "It does not affect me." Then the most important thing I can tell you is that not only does this effect you but also every human on this planet. Not one of us can escape it. We are now going through a "shift" of consciousness, and so is our earth. I have no motive here except to help my fellow humans, my family, and all my friends. I cannot tell you what will happen to you if you fail to awaken and become aware, but I can say it causes great concern in me. Please do not allow yourself to be used, to be played for a fool. We are all in this together. The shift is happening to every single one of us. The spoken word is powerful. I leave you with this mantra, to speak every day: all shift happily now! This was started by the German analyst Tim. It is now being spoken by millions of people worldwide. I realize this may sound "corny" to you, but the idea comes from the Maharishi effect. A collective consciousness saying the same thing not only changes our reality but also has been proven scientifically numerous times worldwide, over decades.

# EPILOGUE

*From the moment I began writing this book, something has been pushing me. It has felt like an unseen force.* I have worked on this book seven days a week, either writing or doing research. Never in my life have I felt so compelled to complete a project. I have pondered this and can only surmise it is because we humans are running out of time. I am only sure of one thing; I have been guided every step of the way.

I am just a man, and there is so much I do not know. However, the one thing I am certain of is that a "shift" is coming. The signs and the evidence are overwhelming.

I must admit, I have had moments where I wanted to reject the things I have learned regarding the UAP presence. I am human, and this information defies the only reality I have ever known. Then I realize that to reject everything would be like saying I know more than most scientist, every elected official in Washington, all the intelligence agencies on Earth, captains of industry, and thousands of researchers who have spent their

lives investigating this subject. I would have to disbe-
lieve every one of the tens of thousands of abductees
and those who have had countless personal interac-
tions with various ET races. I cannot unlearn this vast
amount of knowledge. Furthermore, I know it is fear
inside me that wants to reject these truths.

Early in this book, I spoke of a small group of powerful individuals on this planet who seem to be living
in a parallel reality from the rest of us. They have controlled us, everything we see and hear in the news, and
the vast amount of advanced technology, that has been
withheld from us. Many of us refer to this group as the
Cabal. Others call them the secret world government.
I am happy to report I have learned there are forces at
work to remove this group. Not only have they sold out
humanity but have also been in alliance with the Draco
Reptilians. The Draco have placed installations on Earth
to prevent humanity from conscious evolution. I recently
learned there is now a trial taking place in the Galactic
Federation accusing the Draco of this, which is against
universal law. Specifically, this law is about noninterfer-
ence with any evolving species. The Draco have been
mostly removed from Earth, but they can still affect us
from afar. I am aware this sounds far-fetched, but ancient
history is full of references to Reptilians, in biblical times
and long before. There are so many pieces of artwork,
depicting these beings from thousands of years ago.

There are so many things I do not understand, but
I am convinced we are on the cusp of a major shift in

our reality. Now that the Cabal, and the Draco, are being removed, we will finally get disclosure of the truth. There are literally thousands of researchers, and even government insiders, dreaming of this moment. No one knows exactly how this will unfold, but everyone seems to agree on the following ways we will be affected: we will quickly gain access to free energy and healthcare technology beyond belief. This will expand our lives by at least many decades. It will mean the end of world hunger. Everyone will have a home, built from a new technology. Critically important is that our planet will be cleaned almost overnight. Everyone will have clean water, and the air we breathe will be free of pollution. Poverty will cease to exist, which alone will drop the crime rate by 90 percent the first year. It will suddenly become common to look up and see ET craft flying overhead. We will see extraterrestrials on television, walking on our streets, and being part of our lives. We will have massive exchange programs where graduate students will be sent by the thousands to other civilizations in the galaxy. They will return and write papers on everything they learned from these highly advanced beings. I cannot think of anything in our current reality that will not shift for the better. We will be able to travel anywhere on the planet in minutes. How would you like to join me in Tokyo for dinner tonight? I will have you home by 11:00 p.m.

Our consciousness is evolving now but will shift into the fourth harmonic frequency very soon. With the help of the ETs, we may jump over the fourth and into the fifth density. We will escape the grip of "materialism" in favor of the timeless world of spirit. We will finally remember who we truly are and cease to identify ourselves as our physical bodies. As this occurs, we will truly learn the meaning of loving thy neighbor as thyself. We are all of one consciousness. However, this not only includes all humans but also all sentient life in the universe. This is what the extraterrestrials have been waiting for. We have been fighting and killing each other over nothing. This has largely been so the Cabal could make trillions of dollars from the wars, at least since WWII. Most of us do not want to fight but were tricked into much of it as young men and women. The alien visitors knew we have been told they do not exist and fear anything we do not understand. The truth is we have killed many of them over the years, but still they have not turned hostile toward us.

The reality coming will be beautiful and beyond our imagination. I may not live to see this, but I am completely convinced the shift is imminent. I realize that if this is new to you, it is a lot to wrap your head around. If we had been told the truth years ago, it would not be so shocking. Most of us have lived in ignorance, but this is not our fault. We have been controlled in so many ways. Because the Cabal gained control of most of the news media, and even Hollywood, they controlled the world. I thank God for all those individuals who have spent their lives uncovering the truth, one piece at a time. The whistleblowers risked their lives, and the lives of their families and friends, to shine light on the truth. I pray that one day soon they will receive the full vindication and praise they deserve.

I wrote this book because I am convinced this is the biggest story in the history of the world. I hope it will help you to open your mind and assist in your preparation for what is coming.

With all sincerity, I wish you Godspeed. I ask you to join me daily saying the mantra: *all shift happily now*!

# BIBLIOGRAPHY

Listed below are sources I wish to credit and acknowledge for this book. I have great respect for all, who have spent lifetimes researching their areas of expertise. Without them, much of the content of this book would not have been possible.

The list contains many authors, researchers, scientists from various disciplines, investigative journalists, former intelligence officers, and whistleblowers.

Below is a list of individuals, programs, and books that have provided information and ideals contained in this book:

1. *Chariots of the Gods* by Eric Von Daniken
2. *My Big Toe* by Tom Campbell, Physicist
3. *Selected by Extraterrestrials Vol Two* by William Thompkins
4. *Compendium of the Emerald Tablets* by Billy Carson
5. *Conversations with God* by Neal Donald Walsh
6. *The Day after Roswell* by Lt. Col. Philip Corso

7. *Mass Contact* by Stefano Breccia
8. *The Keys of Enoch* by Dr. J. J. Hurdock
9. *Stranger at the Pentagon* by Dr. Frank Stranges
10. *All the Above ... and Beyond* by Paola Harris
11. *Glimpses of Other Realities* by Linda Moulton Howe
12. *The Akashic Records* by Linda Moulton Howe
13. *Unacknowledged* by Dr. Steven Greer
14. *The Law of One* by Oscar Moya Lledo
15. *The Silva Method of Mind Control* by Jose Silva
16. *Proof of Heaven* by Dr. Eben Alexander, Neurosurgeon on NDEs
17. *Life after Life* by Dr. Raymond Moody, MD, PhD
18. *Sermon on the Mount* by Emmett Fox
19. *The Power of Now* by Eckhart Tolle
20. *The God Man* by C.B Purdom

These are books I have obtained many ideas from. There are so many more I have read over the years. However, most of the information contained in this book was gathered from hundreds of hours watching interviews of many of the authors listed above and countless others. Some came from documentaries such as "The Awakening Mind" but most were from various GAIA-TV programs such as:

1. *Cosmic Disclosure* series
2. *Beyond Belief* with George Noury
3. *Deep Space* series

4. *Ancient Civilizations* series
5. *Wisdom Teachings* series with Davd Wilcock
6. *Open Minds* series with Regina Meridith
7. *Ancient Aliens* series
8. *Disclosure* series with David Wilcock
9. *Mystery Teachings* series with Dr. Teresa Bullard
10. *Ascension Teachings* by William Henry
11. *Sacred Geometry* with Dr. Robert Gilbert PhD
12. *Phenomenon* by James Fox
13. *Bob Lazar: Area 51 and Flying Saucers* documentary
14. *Ascension Keepers*, a series by William Henry
15. *The Bible* series
16. *Drive thru History on the Gospels* series
17. *Drive thru History – Acts to Revelations* series

I have watched hundreds of interviews on these programs, and others. Below are some of the people interviewed, multiple times, I have watched and drawn from in the writing of this book:

1. David Wilcock, author and researcher
2. Emory Smith, former employee of unacknowledged Special Access Program
3. David Adair, physicist, inventor, and many other activities
4. Randy Cramer, alleged member of Secret Space Force

5. Jason Rice, alleged member of Secret Space Force
6. "Tim" the German covert advisor on ET Motives and Agendas
7. Richard Doty, retired Air Force Intelligence officer
8. Linda Moulton Howe, researcher and author
9. Dr. Randy Vietenheimer, expert on energy healing
10. The late Roger Leir, authority on Alien implants and abductions
11. The late Clifford Stone, former Army "Interfacer" with aliens
12. Grant Cameron, known as the "Documents Guy" on UFOs
13. William Henry, mystic researcher and author
14. Paola Harris, field researcher on UFOs
15. Dr. Steven Greer, author and UFO researcher
16. Dr. Robert Wood, aerospace engineer and UFO investigator
17. Billy Carson, researcher and author
18. Eric Von Daniken, author and researcher
19. Dr. Jacque Valle, astronomer and researcher
20. Nick Pope, former British ministry of defense official
21. The late William Thompkins, member of several "think tanks" in the aerospace industry
22. The late Dr. J. Alan Hynek, former scientific

astronomer for Blue Book and UFO researcher

23. Steven Bassett, President of the Paradigm Research Group
24. Jim Self, contactees investigator
25. Jaimie Maussan, Mexican investigative journalist
26. Ricardo Gonzalez, Peruvian author and researcher
27. Dr. Teresa Bullard, physicist
28. Richard Dolan, UFO investigative journalist
29. Bob Lazar, physicist and former Area 51 reverse engineering of alien craft, whistleblower
30. Dr. Alberto Villoldo, PhD, my teacher and mentor on the Shamanic path
31. Jay Weidner, author and researcher on ancient prophecy
32. Dr. Desiree Hurtak, PhD, social scientist
33. Dr. Laura Morrow, PhD, of Think Interfaces
34. Adam Apollo, CEO of Superluminal Systems
35. Matais de Stephano, consciousness educator
36. Giougio A. Tsoukalos, Ancient Aliens
37. Kaedrich Olsen, author on alien species
38. George Knapp, journalist
39. Debbie Solaris, galactic historian
40. Sarah Breskman Cosme, Certified Master Hypnotherapist

41. Craig Campobasso, author of *Alien Species Almanac*
42. Dale Harder, retired former NASA and Honeywell Engineering
43. Dr. Edgar Mitchell, astronaut and UFO researcher
44. Gordon Cooper, astronaut who witnessed UFOs and spoke about the subject
45. Robert Salas, former Air Force officer who testified on UFOs shutting down nuclear missiles
46. Rev. Paul Wallis, Anglican priest from Australia who has researched the UFO topic extensively

# ABOUT THE AUTHOR

Harrison Viers Newberry is an American author. His book *Shining Bear* received only five-star ratings. He has two college degrees, one in medical and the other in environmental health. He has great concerns for our Mother Earth. He arrived late into the literary world, having been a successful businessman for over thirty years. Forty years ago, he began his spiritual journey. He searched for answers to questions we all eventually ask: Who am I? Why am I here? *Imminent Shift* reveals the answers he found. He discovered it was all about consciousness, that we are all one and are connected to all sentient life in the universe.